I0781143

MARRIED TO A DISTINGUISHED THUG 2

SHVONNE LATRICE

About the Author

<u>Other Works by Me:</u>

Good Girls Love Thugs 1-5
Falling for a Hood King 1-4
Married to a Distinguished Thug 1-3
She's Gotta Have It 1-2
Me & My Dope Boy 1-3
Yazir & Nina 1-3
Forbidden Love with a Thug 1-3
You Needed Me 1-3
Shorty is in Love with a Real One 1-4
I Got Your Back 1-2
My Baby Is a West Coast King 1-4
Our Love Is the Realest 1-3
She Got It Bad for a Heartless Gangsta 1-4
She Got It Bad for a Heartless Gangsta: An AK Christmas
Hood Boyz Fall In Love Too 1-3
Nobody Can Love You Like Them Roughnecks Do 1-4
She Gave Her All to the Hood's Finest 1-5

Copyright © 2020 by Shvonne Latrice

All rights reserved.

No part of this book may be reproduced in any form or by any electronic or mechanical means, including information storage and retrieval systems, without written permission from the author, except for the use of brief quotations in a book review.

$14.99
ISBN 978-1-966375-04-3
51499>

KIYUKI ALLEN

„W ait Cori-"

POW!

I ducked quickly, and the bullet shattered my mother's glass vase. *Lord, please let me make it out of here,* I prayed silently. I was too young and sexy to die.

"I trusted you!" Cori screamed as her hands trembled while holding the gun. I knew it was only a matter of time before this bitch tried to kill us all.

"Cori, relax, it's not what you-"

The sound of jingling keys in the door, made us both divert our attention to it. Aniku walked through it, and when she saw Cori pointing a gun at me, her brows furrowed.

"What the fuck is going?" Aniku shouted with a confused expression.

Cori turned and booked it out of the house, shoulder-checking Aniku in the process. I panted for a couple seconds in order to collect my jumbled thoughts. *Was this a dream? Did this bitch really just come in here and try to kill me?* I asked myself as I looked down at my trembling hands.

BOOM!

The sound of Aniku slamming the front door close, snapped me back to reality.

"What the hell Kiyuki?" she frowned.

"What?" I snapped back.

"What the hell are you doing?" She shook her head and threw her hands out.

"What am *I* doing? How about you ask me if I'm okay! That bitch just tried to kill me!" I yelled. I was appalled.

"Why are you even at home? Namiko is in the hospital, and you're here at home painting your fucking nails?" she shouted and gestured towards the nail polish bottle on the coffee table. *Fuck!* I said to myself as I looked down at my fucked up polish.

"Is Namiko all you fucking care about? I'm your fucking sister too, you ungrateful bitch!" I growled.

"Of course I care about you Yuki, but you're acting selfish. You should be by Nami's side right now," she replied in a calmer tone.

"Oh, so forget Kiyuki I see," I scoffed and rolled my eyes.

"No, but I know you Yuki. You did something to that girl." She nodded as if she was so sure.

"You know what? Fuck you Aniku. Fuck you and Namiko's bitch ass! I'm glad she lost her fucking baby!" I smirked. I specifically told those girls to kick Namiko in the stomach, *and* to say Cori sent them.

"She didn't lose the baby. Surprisingly, the baby is in good health." Aniku shook her head at me disappointingly, and stormed to the back.

No! No! I was convinced God was against me. How could the baby be in perfect health? I couldn't wait to get my hands on them stupid hoes that I paid to fuck her up. It was like Namiko and Max had a guardian angel, but I would kill that muthafucka, too, if I had to.

I followed Aniku to the back, because I just couldn't believe what she'd just said.

"Perfect health? How?" I had to ask.

"The doctor said it's a miracle, but the baby is perfectly fine. Namiko will be released in a week," she replied dryly as she stood in the bathroom doorway with her arms folded.

"Why did you even come here? Don't you live with Nami and Max now?" I inquired.

"I came here to find out why you hadn't been to see Namiko, and why you weren't responding to my texts. Now, I'm gonna pee and leave," she spat before slamming the bathroom door in my face. I jumped back to make sure it didn't hit me, and then rolled my eyes.

I went back into the living room, and decided to go make myself a strong ass drink. Ruining what Namiko and Max have, has proven to be far more stressful than anticipated.

As I drank some of my Gin, I looked up at the clock over the sink. Larry was gonna be here in a couple hours, so I still had time to calm myself down.

"What the fuck!" Aniku yelled as she rushed out of the bathroom. Her iPhone was plastered to her ear, as she listened intently to what the caller was saying. "Are they okay?" she panted, as her eyes searched the white walls frantically. I stared at her with my lip turned up, waiting impatiently for her to hang up the damn phone. "Okay, I'm coming back right now," she nodded and pulled her phone away to hang up.

"What happened?" I frowned.

"Max and Deshawn were in a bad accident. We need to go down to St. Johns!" she breathed heavily.

"We? I don't have to do anything. Neither one of them is my man." I laughed wryly and smiled at the memory of setting them up.

"You're such a selfish bitch, Kiyuki. I'm out." Aniku glared at me, and then left the house.

I tried to push her harsh words to the back of my mind, as I drowned myself in some more Gin. All the shit I did for my little sisters, and they decide to turn on me? It was cool though, because no matter how many times I had to try, I would fuck them over for sure. Aniku should've never put herself in this mess, because now my baby sister had to go down too. Hmph, maybe Namiko should be punished for what she did to our father. I laughed at my thoughts as I downed and then refilled my drink.

NAMIKO DAVIS

My body was so sore from that ass whooping I received in that Olive Garden parking lot. When I got to the hospital, I knew for sure that my baby was gone. I cried hysterically, not because of the pain I was in, but because I knew my baby boy was no more.

After I was set up, the doctor let me know my baby was perfectly fine. He said it was a miracle due to the injuries I sustained. I explained to him that after the first kick to the stomach, I blocked the rest. That was probably what saved my baby, in addition to God.

Max said his son was strong, and I agreed, so it was set that we would name him Maximilian Jr. I couldn't wait until he got here, but that was months and months away.

Speaking of Max, he'd left a little while ago to get Evelyn and Aniku something to eat. He should've been back by now, but he wasn't, nor was he answering his phone. I blew out hot air, as Evelyn re-entered my room with a glum look.

"What's wrong?" I slurred.

"Ma-Max and Deshawn were in a really bad car accident Namiko-"

"What! No!" I yelled cutting her off.

"Namiko calm-"

"No! Where is he!" I shouted attempting to get out of bed.

"Nurse!" Evelyn hollered as she tried to restrain me.

"No! Let me go! Where is he?!" I screamed using every bit of strength in my body.

I squirmed wildly, as two nurses rushed into my room. I was like the hulk, as all three ladies tried to pin me to the bed unsuccessfully. They were no match for me at this point, pregnant and all.

"Mrs. Davis, please!" one nurse shouted as she twisted her face up in concern.

"Where is my husband?" I hollered like a wild woman, as I kicked and wiggled my body violently. Next thing I knew, I felt a sharp needle jam into my leg. "Nooo!" I cried and screamed as my body started to become drowsy.

After groggily trying to keep up my wild moves and yells, I drifted off to sleep defeated. I woke up, and I felt extremely sluggish. I slowly looked to my left, and saw my little sister Aniku staring into space.

"Max, where is Max?" I whispered and closed my eyes because it was so bright. Aniku jumped up and ran to my side.

"He's okay. He just broke his leg and bruised himself really badly," she half-smiled as she caressed my hair softly.

I relaxed a little knowing that he was okay. I rubbed my stomach and smiled when I felt my small bump was still present. Ever since Cori had those girls jump me, I was paranoid as hell about losing my baby.

"Deshawn! What about Deshawn?" I asked as I suddenly remembered.

"He's in a coma Nami. He was the driver so he endured most of the impact," she nodded.

Tears welled up in my eyes as I thought about what she said. I hoped he was gonna be okay, because I knew Max and Evelyn would be devastated if he died, and so would I.

"You hungry?" Aniku asked as she continued to caress my head.

I nodded because I was starved. She walked over to me, and opened a McDonald's bag to take out some food. I scarfed down the chicken nuggets before she could even sit them down good. For the first time in my life, I ate every single fry and drank all the pop.

"I want to go see Max now," I said as I started to throw the covers off of me.

"You can't right now. Later on," Aniku replied, putting the blanket back over my bottom half.

"No, now," I whined.

"Namiko, it's 2am. You can't." She shook her head as she set the guest bed up for herself.

"You don't have to sleep here," I said in a low tone.

"I want to," she smiled.

"Has Yuki been here?" I quizzed.

"No, she's tripping right now. Cori pulled a gun out on her," she responded nonchalantly.

"I swear I hate that bitch! She needs to go!" I shouted loudly. What the hell was wrong with her? Was Max that important to where she would kill my sister too?

"Namiko, lower your voice! Relax and read or something," Aniku turned her lip up.

"I'm sorry," I said plopping my head back onto the pillow.

"It's okay, Nami. I know this is a lot to take in. A lot has happened since you've been in here," she scoffed.

"Thank God MJ is okay," I smirked.

"MJ? Already nicknaming him?" she chuckled.

"Yeah," I grinned and palmed my miniature belly. "I can't wait until he gets here," I added.

"Me either. You're gonna be a great mom, just like ours," Aniku smiled.

"You think so?" I wondered.

"I know so Nami. MJ is lucky," she said and we laughed in unison. "I'm gonna have to get used to not thinking about Michael Jackson when we say that," she added and giggled.

"I know," I half-smiled.

I couldn't wait to get out of here and continue my pregnancy. I just needed Deshawn to wake up, and Max to come out of here ASAP. As for Cori, that bitch had it coming. I better not see her, because if I did it was a wrap for her sneaky ass. I was tired of her. She needed to realize that whatever she and Max had was beyond over. I was his wife and a bitch wasn't going no motherfucking where!

MAXIMILIAN DAVIS

A COUPLE DAYS LATER...

Istared at the ceiling of my hospital room just thinking. If I could, I would get up and pace the floor. Everything happened so damn fast. One minute we were being shot at, and the next we were on a one-way street, crashing into an eighteen-wheeler.

I needed to get out of here, and find out who did this shit. A nigga of my caliber could not be sitting up in a hospital in Detroit. Staying here overnight was even risky. I grabbed the beige nurse remote, and pressed the button for assistance.

"Can I help you Mr. Davis?" The nurse radioed in.

"I need someone to come in here with a wheelchair," I said.

"Uh, one moment," she replied. I blew out hot air because I didn't have time for no bullshit. "Mr. Davis, why did you need a chair?" The pretty nurse smiled as she entered my room.

"I want to go see my wife, and then I'm leaving," I responded.

"You can't leave for a couple more days," she blushed. *Why was she blushing?*

"Well, I need to leave right now, after I see my wife."

"Why in such a rush to leave?" she quizzed as she neared me. I tried to sit up, and she helped me do so.

"Let's just say, it's not a good idea for a nigga like me to be laid up in here aight," I exhaled.

"I told them to put you in a different room so that you'd be safe," she said as she shifted her weight from one hip to the other.

"What? Why? You know me?" I frowned.

"Who doesn't know Max Davis?" she snickered and blushed again. I shook my head.

I knew I should've went by a nickname, I thought. I wished I could go back ten years and decide not to go by Max. When I first got started, I declined to use a nickname due to the simple fact niggas thought it was an alias anyway, because it wasn't likely that a nigga from Detroit, Michigan was named Max or even worse Maximilian. On top of that, only hood muthafuckas knew I provided drugs for the whole city of Detroit, Flint, and a couple other surrounding areas. Everybody else thought I was just some rich ass club owner, and I wanted to keep it that way. I didn't need the police coming for me, or watching me at all. Me being black alone was a reason enough for them to suspect me of something.

"Well, then you know a brother needs to get out," I replied running my hand over my fade.

"I'm not supposed to, but for you I will," she smiled and bit her bottom lip.

"Thanks Melissa," I said as I read her name badge.

She chuckled and ran her happy ass out to get me a wheelchair. I looked around the room, and realized I'd lost my phone in the midst of the crash. Thank God I didn't handle business with my personal phone, because that would be all bad if it was confiscated.

"Okay!" Melissa beamed as she wheeled a chair in for me. She rushed over to help me stand up, and the back of my gown came open, exposing my bare ass.

"Nice," she commented and I frowned. "I can bathe you when we get back," she offered. As bad as I didn't want her thirsty ass to, I agreed because I needed it.

After telling her where Namiko was, she wheeled me to her room. When we entered, Aniku was leaving.

"I'm gonna be back after class," Aniku smiled. I smiled to myself, because she was happy as hell to be in college.

I nodded at her and then locked my eyes on my beautiful wife. Her dark caramel skin was bruised, but still looked smooth and just as perfect as before. Her slanted eyes had small bruises around them, and her full bottom lip was busted.

"Closer," I whispered to Melissa. She pushed me closer, and then I palmed Namiko's stomach. She jumped and looked over at me, then grinned.

"Max!" she hopped up and plopped in my lap.

"Uh!" I grunted in pain.

"I'm sorry baby, I just missed you," she smiled and kissed all over my face.

Beat up and all, Namiko was a twenty out of ten. I grabbed her face and kissed her lips. We kissed for a nice little while, until I felt Melissa adjust her grip on the handles of the wheelchair.

"Can you give us a minute?" I asked looking up at her.

"I will be back in four minutes flat. We need to bathe you and make sure you can check out," she winked and switched off.

"She needs to get a bigger uniform," Namiko spat.

"Why?" I chuckled.

"It's too tight! Her boobs and ass are busting out!" she exclaimed. "Do you see me walking around like that?" she frowned.

"No, but you've worn some pretty tight shit. That's why you had a nigga being celibate for almost a year." I bit my lip and eyed her in that hospital gown as if it were lingerie.

I rubbed my hand up her gown, and smiled when I realized she was naked underneath, like me. I lifted her up, and then brought her down onto my dick slowly.

"Ooooh," we whispered in unison.

I sucked her lips as she bounced on my dick very slowly. Her pussy was feeling too good and tight, and I knew I would be nutting any minute. I didn't mind though, because Melissa would be back in a couple.

"I'm cumming Max!" Namiko howled softly.

"Shhhh. Oooh fuck," I grunted as I felt my dick harden even more, signaling that I would be releasing soon.

"Ahhhh!" we both called out as we exploded together.

"That was the quickest nut in life. That's how you know your pussy is good," I panted as Namiko's pussy throbbed around my dick.

"Okay, times up." Melissa walked in.

Namiko's eyes got big because I was still inside her. I wanted to go for another round, but that wasn't an option due to Melissa being back, and the fact that my leg was starting to hurt. Namiko got up slowly, and quickly jumped in the bed. My dick was exposed and glistening, so I quickly covered it. Melissa promptly spun me around, and pushed me back to my room. When we got there, I saw she had a hospital bucket filled with soapy water waiting for me. She closed the door, and then helped me to the bathroom where we removed my gown.

"Make this quick," I demanded.

"Yes sir," she smirked as she paid extra attention to my abs, with her eyes locked on my dick that was still slowly going down.

KIYUKI

I woke up to the sound of someone pressing down on the doorbell. I could barely sleep anyway, because I was worried about finding a way to pay this damn mortgage. I refused to kiss Namiko's ass so that she could pay it, and I knew there was now way Max would rehire me.

I looked at the clock and saw it was 10am. I was surprised I even slept that late. I padded to the door, and took a deep breath before twisting the knob. Before it was open good, Larry rushed in.

"Why you ain't been to see your sister?" he asked.

"Uh, because I don't like that bitch," I scoffed as I locked the front door.

"Kiyuki, we set Max and Deshawn up. We don't need them looking at us as possible suspects. If they know you're upset, they're gonna look at you as a possibility. Then after you, they're gonna look at me," he explained.

"So what are you telling me?" I raised a brow.

"I'm telling you to go visit your sister," he huffed.

"This is bullshit. I don't want to see her!"

"Do you want to die Yuki? Do you know who we're up against?" he frowned.

"Let's just leave town!" I shouted.

"Leave town? You think we can just leave town and it'll be over? This is Max Davis, Kiyuki! Plenty of niggas would've just left town if they could." He turned his lip up at me in disappointment.

I was starting to get scared and I wasn't before. I knew Max could be ruthless, but I thought for some reason he would never find out it was Larry and I who had them shot at.

"So just play nice?" I asked.

"Yes, for now. I need to think of a way we can plant this shit on someone else. If Max finds the guys who shot at him and Deshawn, they're sure to run their fucking mouths." He shook his head. I'd never seen Larry this scared in his life.

"Why would you use them?" I yelled. Who would purposely use niggas that may snitch?

"I only hired one fucking guy, and he went ahead and implemented his friends! I don't know them other niggas Yuki, and I didn't expect Max and Deshawn to make it out alive." He exclaimed.

"You're so fucking stupid!" I shouted.

"Don't do that! This ain't the fucking time to be doing that shit, aight? We need to stick together!" he shouted back. I just shook my head at him because he was definitely the dumbest nigga I'd ever met. I should've never conspired with him.

After Larry left, I hopped in the shower and got dressed to go see Namiko. I got to the hospital in no time, and took my sweet time walking in. I needed to gather my thoughts so that I could play the concerned big sister role.

"Hello, I'm here to see Namiko Allen," I fake smiled at the receptionist nurse.

"Mm, we don't have a Namiko Allen." She shook her head as she looked at the computer. I exhaled and rolled my eyes.

"Davis. Namiko Davis," I rephrased.

"Okay, we did have a Namiko Davis but she checked out," she smiled.

I smacked my lips, and then switched my sexy ass back to the parking lot. I was gonna give up, but I thought about what Larry said. My life depended on this shit, and I needed to suck it up.

I drove to the mansion that she and Max lived at, and pulled up to the gate. *When did they get this shit?* I wondered referring to the gate.

"Can I help you?" the security asked.

"I'm here to visit my sister, Namiko," I replied nastily. Who the fuck was he to question me?

"One moment," the stocky muthafucka spat, and walked to his booth like he had molasses in his ass.

"Can you hurry up?" I shouted and honked. He ignored me and continued to walk like a snail. He came back out after what felt like one hundred years, and knocked so hard on my window I thought it would shatter. "Damn nigga-"

"Go in!" he yelled cutting me off as the big gates parted.

"Bitch," I said under my breath as I drove through.

I parked my Mercedes that may soon be confiscated if I didn't get my hands on some money, and then walked up to the door. *This house is so beautiful,* I thought as I waited for the door to be answered.

"Hi," Namiko smiled as she pulled the door back.

She had on a tight, short sleeved dress, fuzzy socks, and her long dark hair was in a ponytail that cascaded down her back. I would be lying if I said I didn't somewhat miss her pretty face. As much as I hated her, I loved her. How could I not, she was my little sister.

"Hi babe," I fake smiled and walked in to hug her. Her belly bump poked me a little, and suddenly I felt bad that I had tried to kill my niece or nephew. Once that baby got here, I may not ever be able to look it in the face.

"What is it?" I asked rubbing her small stomach.

"A boy," she grinned and I nodded. She was so happy, and the guilt was really starting to pour into my soul.

"Come on." She waved me over to follow her to the humongous kitchen.

I looked around in awe before sitting down. I'd only seen the foyer and bedroom in the past.

"That smells good," I commented as she turned the heat on the stove down.

"Thanks. It's fried chicken, yams, macaroni, and creamed spinach," she replied as she worked her way around.

"Wow. Planning to blow up," I scoffed.

"Well, I am eating for two, and plus, Aniku and Max eat a lot," she said. I rolled my eyes since her back was turned. "Did you want to stay and eat?" she offered.

"No," I replied. "I need you to talk to Max about rehiring me Nami. I don't know how I'm gonna pay my car note or the mortgage," I said.

"I can't tell Max what to do, Yuki," she responded without looking at me.

"Wow. All you care about is yourself." I shook my head.

"Really? Even though I just invited my sister who tried to sleep with my man, to dinner? That sounds pretty selfless to me! You're lucky I didn't beat your ass when you walked in!" she glared at me.

"Whoa, what's going on?" Max asked as he used his crutches to walk in.

"Yuki wants her job back," Namiko said staring at me.

"Don't get upset like that with my son in there." Max palmed her stomach and towered over her to kiss her lips. She smiled and pecked him again before he left the kitchen. I guess the fact that he completely ignored her statement, meant me getting my job back was out the window.

"Listen Yuki, if you find something to do, I will pay for your mortgage and car until you get on your feet. Go to school or something," she said.

"No. I'm not going to school. I don't need this advice you're giving. I need money," I said standing up. "You're lucky, you bagged a baller," I added.

"Yeah I did, but that's just by the grace of God. I love Max and it has nothing to do with his money. Please don't forget that I have one more year of college left before I start on my masters, so in the end, I will have money with or without Max. That's what you need to do. And if you hadn't been such a hoe, you'd still have your job," she spat as she placed some glasses in the freezer to frost.

My stomach growled as the food aroma hit my nose. "I'm gonna stay and eat," I said disregarding her lecture. Plus, I needed to stay on her and Max's good side.

NAMIKO

I'd been keeping my ear to the streets as they say, looking for Cori. I'd even hidden out at Red Sugar to see if I could catch that hoe. Yeah Kiyuki was a selfish hoe, but she was my sister. No bitch had any business pulling a gun out on her. Aniku thought I was crazy, and she said that this baby was to blame. I kind of agreed, but then again Cori had fucked with me so much, that it was only right she'd turn me a little crazy.

"Babe, does Cori not work for Red Sugar anymore?" I asked Maximilian.

"Nami, stop worrying about that girl. Nobody knows where she has run off to," he said fixing his tie. "Deshawn and I been looking for her too," he added as he looked into the mirror to make sure the tie was right. My baby insisted on taking me out to dinner, even though he had to use crutches.

"I look fat," I pouted and hunched my shoulders over in the full-length mirror.

"No you don't babe. And you're only almost five months. You're gonna get bigger, right?" Max reminded me.

"Yep, and I'm gonna be on bedrest because I refuse to go out looking like a whale," I said as I did a 360-degree spin.

Max strutted over to me, looking so good in his Tom Ford suit. He wrapped his strong arms around me from behind, and let his dark caramel hands palm my stomach.

"You're beautiful," he said slightly above a whisper. I stared into the mirror at his beautiful face, and got lost. Even though we'd been together for a while, I still felt the same as I did when we first met. His beautiful looks were almost blinding. He was too good to be true sometimes. "Aight, come on," he said smacking my ass.

"Ow," I whined.

As we walked through the foyer, Aniku came running through it to the kitchen. I was about to speak but changed my mind. As we were walking out, Konz was walking into the house.

"Aye nigga, where the fuck is your phone?" he frowned as he closed the front door behind him.

"In my pocket," Max responded as he pulled it out to see a missed call from his brother. I peeped a couple bitches' names on the screen too, but I declined to say anything right now.

"What did you want?" Max asked.

"I need yo' fucking Netflix password. That shit signed me out!" Konz shook his head.

"Nigga, you drove to my crib for my Netflix password?" Max asked and I laughed.

"Yeah nigga! I got a little something something at the crib, and I'm trying to do that whole Netflix and chill shit," Konz licked his lips. Max shook his head, and pulled out his phone to text the password to Konz.

"And don't give my shit to them rats you be dealing with," Max spat as he slipped his phone back into his pocket.

"Hey Aniku," Konz smirked as my little sister strutted by.

"Hey Konz," she blushed.

"When we gone chill?" He grinned and threw his hands out. *Oh hell nah!* I thought.

"Um, never," I chimed in.

"Come on sister and law! You got my brother, let me have your sister," Konz chuckled.

"It's sister *in* law you damn fool," Max corrected him and we all laughed.

"Man, whatever. Hit me up Aniku!" Konz smiled and put his hand into the shape of a phone before leaving. I shot Aniku a look, and she just giggled and ran up the stairs to her room.

"Aniku is smart, she knows not to fuck with my little bro," Max chuckled and so did I. I hoped she was smart enough, because I didn't want my sister giving up the goods before marriage.

Max took me to Cliff Bells, and I fell in love with the Cotton Club feel it had.

"You know I still like the regular places," I smiled, after the waiter set our drinks down.

"I know, and that's all the more reason why you deserve to come to places like this." He bit his lip. I smiled because he knew me so well.

"So how is it being married Mrs. Davis?" he smirked, and I melted at the sound of him calling me that, even though I heard it all day.

"It's okay," I joked and he nodded with his mouth open. "You know I'm kidding buttercup," I giggled, and he shook his head.

"You can't be calling me that in public," he cheesed.

"Why? You don't want people to know that Maximilian Davis' nickname is buttercup?" I said cracking up. It was so hilarious how he was tough as nails, yet I called him that. I specifically chose that name because it was super cheesy, and because his smooth dark caramel skin was like butter.

"Hell nah! You out here calling me a stripper name!" he said, and I burst into laughter.

"It's not a stripper name, babe. It's the name of the toughest Powerpuff girl," I said as I laughed.

"Now how the fuck is that any better? I don't even know what a powderpuff girl is, but it don't sound like nothing I would be," he chuckled as I doubled over in laughter.

"My back hurts!" I whined as I chuckled. "What would you rather me call you?" I asked wiping tears from my eyes.

"Thug nasty," he nodded and we laughed.

"That's dumb as fuck Max. That's a stripper name," I smiled at him.

"But at least it's a male stripper name and not that powder puff shit you was talking about.

"It's power-puff not powder," I cheesed.

"I hate you," he replied.

"You love me," I smirked.

"You're right," he said licking his lips.

"I'm so happy I took that job working for you. I may not have ever met you," I said on a serious note.

"Yes you would've," he responded, as he moved back a little to let the waiter set the appetizer down.

"How so?" I quizzed.

"Because we were meant to be. If we didn't meet that way, we would've met another way," he nodded as if he was so sure.

"You're such a charmer," I smiled.

"I guess." He shrugged and popped his collar.

"You know you are. You charmed me right out of my panties too," I chuckled.

"Did I?" he raised a brow.

"Yes! I'd never let a guy see me naked, or give me head," I furrowed my brows.

"Well see, it's just a gift I have," he grinned.

"It is."

"And now, you're stuck with this dick forever." He raised both of his eyebrows repeatedly.

"I don't mind. I'm sure it's the best," I replied.

"Nami, you better stop before I take you out to the car," he said and I knew he was dead serious, because there was no sign of a smile on his face.

After dinner, we went to the Redford Theatre to see an old movie. Tonight they were playing *The Night of the Hunter*, a film from 1955, and I was so anxious to see it since we'd bought our tickets prior. Old movies were one of the things that Max and I loved in common.

"I wish you could massage my feet, but that arm is bruised up," I said as I took off my dress in the bedroom.

"Oh, my bad," he replied sarcastically and I giggled.

We climbed in bed together, and I sat between his legs as he massaged my stomach. Midway through *Love and Hip Hop*, I reached back and dipped my hand into his boxers. I leaned my head back, and Max pressed his lips against mine.

"I turned you out," he smiled, flashing his perfect white teeth.

"You did," I replied, as I continued to massage his dick, which was now brick hard.

I turned around and pulled his t-shirt material boxer briefs down. I took his beautiful dick into my mouth, and bobbed up and down on it. I never thought I would be able to say I liked sucking dick, but I did.

"Ahhh," Max moaned softly. I loved to hear him moan. He ran his hand down my back, and unhooked my bra. "Damn Namiko," he panted as I massaged his balls. My saliva covered him completely, as I let the head of his ten inches bump my tonsils. "I love when you do that shit," he commented, referring to me letting his dick sit in my throat for a couple seconds. "I'm cumming Nami." He grunted as he hit the pillow next to him. I sped up, and looked up into his eyes. He came soon after, and I swallowed every drop.

He lightly picked my head up, and slid himself down. "Sit on my face," he demanded.

I removed my panties, and then climbed his perfect physique. I sat on his face, and he took my clit into his mouth. He sucked hungrily, as I rocked my hips slowly.

"Max," I cooed as he used his good hand to smack and grab my ass cheeks.

"Bounce up and down," he ordered. "Slow," he added.

I did as he asked, and every time I came down slowly, he sucked the life out of my pearl. It was crazy how he knew just what to do, and it always made me cum hard.

"What are you doing to me Max?" I whimpered as I clutched my sweaty hands onto the headboard. I looked down with a confused expression, because he was eating my pussy way too good. I rained down on his mouth and he kept attacking. I ground my pussy against his mouth, and he took every stroke. My buttercup was a beast. Ha ha.

"Ahhh. Maaaxxx I-Ahhh," I cried out as I came again. I was spent, my pregnant ass couldn't take all this.

"I want you to ride it for daddy," he commanded. I slid my soaking wet pussy down onto his dick, and began to ride him slowly. "You can't hang, mommy?" he asked, biting his lip. He squeezed my trembling legs, as I tried my best to ride him, although tired. He sat up and flicked his tongue over my hard nipples, as he gripped my ass cheeks. "I got you. Get on your back," he smiled, referring to me being tired.

"Your arm, Max," I whined.

"Woman, get on your back so I can fuck you. Don't worry about this cast. I'm a G," he said as he lightly pushed me onto my back. He slid back inside me, and fucked the living day lights out of me. "Got damn you got some voodoo," he panted as he made me cum for the fourth time.

He lifted my leg with his good arm, and pumped me in a circular motion. It felt way too good, and I knew I would soon be cumming again. The sight of him humping me, and his biceps flexing, was sexy as hell.

"This is about to be a heavy load Nami," he commented and scrunched his sexy face up.

"Uhhhhh!" he grunted as he released into me. I came on his dick seconds after, and he dipped his tongue into my mouth. "Nami, you better not ever let no nigga try this shit out. This will make niggas crazy," he panted as he kissed all over my sweaty face and neck.

"This is only for you," I reminded him, as I enjoyed the soft kisses he planted on me. I loved this man.

MAXIMILIAN

A COUPLE WEEKS LATER....

Today, I was going to see my boy Deshawn. He was still out cold, and that shit bothered me. I was gonna dedicate lengthy hours to finding out who was behind this shit. The longer it took the bigger price they'd have to pay.

I adjusted my hat and headed into the hospital. When I walked into Deshawn's room, he was laying there looking dead. He was attached to all these different machines, and a tube was shoved down his throat. I sat down next to him, and dropped my face into my hands for a couple seconds. I didn't know what I would do if my homie died. We grew up together, and he was just as much a brother as Konz. I couldn't believe Cori hadn't stopped by to see him. Then again, she didn't even know he was out cold. Even Robbie's bitch ass had been by to see him.

"We need you to wake up, bro," I finally spoke. The only sound coming from him was the machines. After chilling with him for an hour, I was about to leave so I could go do some hood research.

"Hey Mr. Davis," my old nurse walked in smiling.

"Hey... Melissa," I half smiled, after checking her nametag again.

"You forgot my name," she smacked her lips and grinned.

"Nah, of course not," I lied. "Are you Deshawn's nurse too?" I frowned.

"No, this isn't my area. I just came to see how you were doing," she blushed.

"How did you know I was here?" I asked.

"I checked the check-in counter downstairs," she nodded. *Who does that?* I wondered.

"Right. Well nice seeing you," I said patting her on the shoulder.

"You know if you need some therapy for your limbs I can help," she offered.

"What are you really trying to do here?" I raised a brow.

"Excuse me?" she asked, folding her arms across her breasts. She reminded me of that video vixen Rosa Acosta. In other words, she was bad as hell.

"What are you trying to do? Why do you care so much about how I'm doing?" I quizzed.

"Because I'm a nurse," she giggled.

"Okay," I said and walked out the room. She power walked after me, and once she caught up, she started walking with me.

"Because I like you," she answered.

"I thought so," I said and continued to walk out.

"So what now?" she called out after me.

"You met my wife," I shrugged and left.

I hated hoes like that. She knew I was married, and still wanted to be down. I shook my head at the thought.

"Max!" Evelyn called out as I jogged out the hospital.

"Oh hey," I smiled and gave her a hug. I was happy to see that Deshawn had finally found someone. Evelyn was a winner just like Namiko, so he didn't have to worry about her being some gold digger.

"How long do you usually stay?" I inquired.

"Pretty much all day long, until I need a good night's sleep, or I have to leave for class," she forced a smile.

"Damn. Well don't trip Ev, he's gonna wake up soon," I assured her, although I had no idea. She nodded and then headed inside.

I wanted to have Deshawn attended to by a personal nurse, because I felt uneasy leaving him here overnight. However, I knew they wouldn't let us take him out. We'd have to kidnap him, and I didn't feel like dealing with that. I, however, had someone on the inside watching him and making sure anybody outside of Evelyn, Robbie, and I were not allowed into his room. That made me feel a little better about leaving him here.

I drove to my office that I had inside of a rundown warehouse. No one knew what was in there, unless they'd visited me there before. I was meeting some of my hood soldiers, to see if they had any information for me on the people who shot at Deshawn and I.

"So what's up?" I asked as I sat down behind my desk.

"We think we know who shot at y'all, but we need a little more time to be sure," my boy Corbin replied.

"How much more time? I can do this shit myself," I said shaking my head.

"Nah, we got it man! I promise!" he replied.

I shook my head because I wasn't sure if I should leave this in their hands. Whenever a muthafucka took too long to bring me some shit, I always got frustrated and took over. Maybe I needed to just allow them to complete the job. When I was heavy in the streets, pushing dope and robbing niggas, an enemy of mine didn't make it overnight. I didn't play that shit. I couldn't sleep until that nigga was in the ground.

"But Max, we're pretty sure it was a group of niggas who were hired to take you out," another soldier named Quinton chimed in. *Hired?* I thought.

This is the second time some shit like this has happened. I bet it was Cori's ass. I'd been way too lenient with her, so now I needed to keep an eye on her. If I found out she had done this drive by shit too, I was killing her ass off top!

"Damn, so an inside job," I scoffed and everyone nodded.

"Alright, well y'all got two fucking weeks! Just two! If I don't have any names or heads on platters, I'm doing the shit myself and terminating y'all," I said standing up. I meant every word too. I didn't have time for the bullshit!

KIYUKI

„Why the fuck are you over here?" I pouted as I sat in Larry's passenger seat.

"We about to go visit Deshawn," he replied cranking his car up.

"What? Why?" I snapped my neck towards him.

"I already told your ass why!" he shouted. I rolled my eyes and buckled my seat belt.

I was never one to be fake, so I hated all this bullshit Larry suggested that we do. We arrived at St. Johns Hospital, and went straight towards the front desk.

"Yeah uh, we are here to see Deshawn Sinead," Larry told the nurse.

"What is your name?" she asked.

"I'm Larry," he replied as I filed my nails not giving a fuck. He told me to stay by the door, and wait for his cue to come with him.

"You're not on the list to see him," the lady replied as she scrolled on her computer.

"Okay, let me make a call," Larry said and walked back towards me so we could go outside.

"Well, looks like we need to leave," I chuckled, happy that this mission had failed.

"No, we need to think of something," he replied and paced the ground outside.

"Oh my gosh! I don't want to see that nigga! I'm hungry, lets go!" I spat.

"Look, I don't know about you, but I value my life. If we don't visit this nigga we gon' look suspicious! I don't want Max thinking I have any ill feelings about him firing me!" Larry yelled in my face. I mushed him back, and then leaned up against the brick wall of the hospital. "What's his girlfriend's name?" Larry asked as if he had a bright idea.

"Evelyn. Why?" I shrugged and rolled my eyes at the thought of her.

"Go inside Evelyn," he smiled.

"What? She comes here all the time! They gonna know I ain't her!" I barked but in a low tone.

"Just try it," Larry said, turning me around and shoving me through the sliding doors.

"What about you?" I frowned.

"Just tell them it's okay for me to come in," he responded.

"What if that doesn't work?" I quizzed. This shit was so stupid.

"If she says no, just go and visit him for a bit. Anything is good for now," he smiled. I shook my head, then went back inside and over to the desk.

"Hi, since you said my friend can't come in under his name, can he come with me?" I smiled.

"What is your name?" she raised a brow. I paused for a second so I could remember Evelyn's last name.

"Evelyn Turner," I nodded.

"Do you have your ID?" she asked. *Think fast Kiyuki.*

"I come here every fucking day, and y'all never ask me for no fucking ID! All I want is to see my damn man! I don't have time for this shit!" I screamed.

"Ma'am, this is procedure. We have to check ID," the receptionist whined.

"I don't give a fuck about procedure! Give me a fucking visitor's pass so I can be on my fucking way! You don't want it with me bitch!" I shouted as a white man jogged over.

"Rachel, what's the problem?" he asked.

"The problem is, my nigga is laid up there in a coma and she won't let me see him! I'm about to turn this muthafucking hospital out!" I hollered before Rachel could respond. "I come here every fucking day! Y'all should recognize me by now," I added.

"Does she?" the white guy asked. Rachel, the receptionist, scrolled on her computer and then nodded to say yes.

"Okay Ms. Turner, we are gonna let you go this once, but please have your ID ready for any future visits," he said writing "my name" on a badge and handing it over. I snatched it and pinned it to my tube top.

"Can my friend come?" I asked again.

"Not if he isn't on the list Ms. Turner," the white guy replied. I rolled my eyes and headed up to Deshawn's room.

Me: *You can't come in.*

I text Larry.

Larry: *okay, just chill for like an hour.*

Me: *An hour? Nigga no!*

I replied and locked my phone. I strutted down the hall, and saw about five nurses leaving Deshawn's room. *Lord, please don't let him be dead, or Max may kill all of Detroit,* I said in my head. It was fine if we killed them both, but not just one because I was not in the mood for that level retaliation.

I walked into the room, and Deshawn was awake. Fuck! I was expecting to sit here and be on my phone while he was dead to the world. *Shit, he saw me so I can't back out,* I told myself.

"Kiyuki?" he asked with a scratchy voice. His already light skin looked pale, and his curly hair was dry. I swear he looked just like Quincy, P. Diddy's stepson.

"Hey," I said dryly, and lazily lifted my hand up to wave.

"Wh-why are you here?" he frowned his cute face.

"I just wanted to make sure you were okay. I'm happy to see that you're awake. When did this happen?" I inquired.

"Two days ago," he half smiled.

"I see. Well let me go. You probably want to be alone," I chuckled.

"Nah, stay please. I'm bored," he pleaded. Fuck.

"Okay," I smiled and sat back down.

Surprisingly, Deshawn and I had good conversation, and I lost track of time. I had been with him for three hours so far.

"I've been here for hours!" I laughed.

"I know. Thank you, I appreciate it," he smirked. *Damn, he's kind of sexy,* I thought to myself.

"Well, maybe I can come back to see you tomorrow," I offered.

"Yeah, that'd be nice. I don't get out until next Friday," he exhaled.

"Sounds-"

"I'm the only fucking Evelyn! What bitch do y'all have in my nigga's room?" Evelyn hollered in the hallway. *Aww shit, here we go*, I said to myself as I stood up.

Deshawn sat up in the bed, as Evelyn and two nurses burst through. "Kiyuki? Bitch you better step!" Evelyn shouted and pointed to the door. I couldn't help but laugh at her stupid ass.

"See you later Deshawn," I winked to piss Evelyn off.

As soon as I got in the hallway, I heard her going in on Deshawn, and the nurses were trying to calm her down. My phone started to ring, and I saw it was Larry. I'd forgotten all about him. I walked outside and he was yelling on my voicemail as I approached him.

"What the fuck? I said one hour!" he shouted.

"I wanted to make a good impression. He's awake, by the way." I smiled and opened the door on the passenger side.

"Stupid bitch," Larry mumbled.

I needed to figure out a way to disassociate myself from Larry. That way, when all this shit hit the fan, he'd be drowning alone.

NAMIKO

Today I was going shopping for my son's nursery. Although I was excited for my baby to come, I was a little worried that my last year of college would be unsuccessful. How was I gonna take care of a baby, *and* finish school. I didn't even want to think about the master's program I needed to complete.

"Stop being negative Namiko," I said as I brushed my edges.

"Negative about what?" Max asked as he entered my vanity room.

"Umm, the-"

"Nami," he said and made a face to let me know not to lie.

"About the baby," I replied and stared into his eyes to see if he was upset. He walked over to me, and leaned down to kiss my lips.

"Why would you have negative thoughts about the baby?" he inquired.

"Not necessarily the baby, but being a mommy and going to school. I don't want to use a nanny," I replied.

"I'm gonna help you, Nami, and there is nothing wrong with a nanny if you do it right," he chuckled.

"I know, but dads can only do so much," I frowned.

"We each have separate roles. You're there to nurture him and show him love. I'm here to show him how to be a man and love him.

We can do this if we work together. I don't mind doing something if you need to do homework or study," he smiled.

"You don't?" I quizzed. I wasn't used to this. My mom and dad were very old fashioned, so my dad didn't change diapers or anything like that.

"Baby, what do you think, I'm a caveman? It's my responsibility as his father to help you," he grinned. I stood up and draped my arms around his neck.

"You always know what to say," I said staring into his eyes. "I love you so much, Max. Don't you ever fall in love with anyone else," I smirked.

"I couldn't," he replied and kissed me. "Tell your mommy to stop acting like she don't have a husband," he said to my belly and kissed it.

"You look nice, where are you going?" I asked Max. He always looked sexy though. He wore dark jeans, a navy blue t-shirt with a little pocket on the left side, a black cap, and some black and navy blue Nikes. His cologne was intoxicating as usual.

"To handle some business," he shrugged.

"You never tell me what handling business is." I folded my arms.

"Because you don't need to know," he said and pecked my lips before leaving.

❦

"Grab a basket," I said to Evelyn as we walked into Target.

"You have a basket Nami."

"I'm gonna need two," I cheesed, and she shook her head.

"So guess who was chilling in Deshawn's room while I was in class?" Evelyn exhaled as we looked at baby cribs.

"No idea," I replied.

"Kiyuki. She pretended to be me, and was in there with him," she spat.

"I'm sure she was just being nice," I said even though I was a little perplexed as well. Evelyn and Kiyuki hated each other as it is, so anything I could say to diffuse the situation would be said.

"Nami, the only time she's nice to a guy is when she's hoping to hop on that dick." Evelyn shook her head.

"Well, what did Deshawn say?" I inquired.

"That she was just keeping him company," she scoffed and gave me a face like *yeah right*.

"Well, until we get some confirmation, we can't really accuse her of anything."

"I hope she's just being nice because I would hate to have to kill your sister *and* Deshawn," she said and we laughed.

Once we loaded everything into the car, with the help of the store sales associate, I was ready to go home and pig out.

"He gets out tomorrow, let's swing by and see if she's there," Evelyn suggested.

"Isn't there a list? How would she get by, now that they know she's not you?" I quizzed.

"I just want to see Namiko," she responded and headed in the direction of the hospital.

We checked in at the front, and we were issued badges after showing our IDs. They tried to give me a hard time, until some Melissa chick informed them that I was Max's wife. I don't know how she knew that, but then again she did look familiar.

"This is it," Evelyn smirked as we neared Deshawn's room. To my surprise, Kiyuki was in here helping Deshawn eat. "Are you serious Deshawn?" Evelyn folded her arms over her chest, as Kiyuki rolled her eyes.

"Calm down Ev, it ain't even like that." Deshawn sighed and shook his head.

"Nigga, what the fuck you shaking your head for? I should be shaking mine!" Evelyn shouted.

"Evelyn relax, you can't be yelling in here," I said.

"Namiko, this is none of your business." She quickly shut me down while looking over her shoulder.

"Why do you always have to blow up and shit for no damn reason?" Deshawn frowned.

"Because you always doing some shit!" she yelled back.

"I'm out," Kiyuki said and grabbed her purse.

"Why are you looking like you wanna stop her?" Evelyn questioned Deshawn.

"Man, shut up," he waved her off, and she charged his ass.

"Evelyn!" I shouted as Kiyuki and I pulled her off of Deshawn.

"You three are gonna have to leave." A nurse entered the room as Evelyn snatched her arm from Kiyuki. We all paused for a couple seconds, and then left the room like the nurse asked.

"I bet not catch you sniffing around my nigga," Evelyn threatened Kiyuki.

"I think he's sniffing around me," Kiyuki chuckled and switched off.

"I swear Nami," Evelyn inhaled.

"Calm down Evelyn, we didn't see anything. Let's go eat so you can calm down and I can stuff my face," I half smiled.

"No, I'm staying here," she frowned.

"Ev-"

"I'm not about to let your sister take my man, Namiko," she cut me off sternly.

"Okay." I power walked until I caught up to Kiyuki, and I was tired as hell by the time I reached her.

"Can I have a ride to get some food and then home?" I asked since Evelyn was my original ride. Evelyn would just have to drop off the stuff I bought from Target later.

"What are you gonna do for me?" she smiled. "Kiyuki! Please, I'm pregnant and I'm hungry!" I whined and tears started to well up. Yes, I was crying because I was hungry.

"Fine," she scoffed and rolled her eyes.

She took me to Popeyes so I could get a three-piece wing meal, and the five-piece chicken strips meal, and yes I wanted both of my drinks.

"Thanks for the food," she said when we got back into the car.

"You're welcome," I replied as I tapped my leg impatiently. I wanted to get home and eat. After a couple minutes of silence, I finally broke it. "Yuki, are you messing around with Deshawn?" I questioned.

"How could I? He's in the hospital," she smirked.

"Yuki."

"No, okay? I was just being nice. He gets lonely and bored when little miss Evelyn is in class. Max comes but he can never stay past an hour. And as you know, I have no job so I have all the time in the world," she scoffed and shook her head.

"I see," I replied in a low tone.

I believed her and I hoped she wasn't pulling the wool over my eyes. I wanted my sister to change so badly, but she was just so corrupted. She had always been harsh with her words ever since we were little kids, so that was nothing new. She was a straight shooter and always spoke her mind, but her behavior seemed to be slightly off now. I'm not sure where my parents went wrong, because Aniku and I came out just fine. I barely said bye, as I hopped out of the car and rushed inside to scarf down my meals.

MAXIMILIAN

While Evelyn was in class, I was gonna go pick up my boy, Deshawn from the hospital. Robbie could've done it, but that nigga had been MIA just like his fucking sister.

"Hurry up Max, so we can get this nigga and go smoke!" Konz spat.

"Nigga, what else do you do besides smoke?" I frowned as I opened my fresh pair of Jordan Retro 7's.

"I told yo' ass I got a hustle," he chuckled.

That nigga sure hadn't been asking me for any money for the past month. I don't know how I didn't notice.

"Oh yeah? What's that?" I asked as I tied my shoe.

"Don't trip. Just know I'm getting that bread and with bread comes bitches," he grinned and I shook my head.

"Is it legal?" I looked at him.

"Nigga is what *you* doing legal?" he snapped.

"Some parts, yeah. Red Sugar, and the eight Popeyes franchises I own are all the way legal," I chuckled.

"Fuck you," he spat as I put on my white Bermuda Kangol hat.

"Come on nigga," I said slapping his shoulder, and walking out of the bedroom.

"Fuck off me," he mumbled and I chuckled at his angry ass.

When we got there, Deshawn was ready and packed up. He was walking pretty normal except for a slight limp. We all decided we would go chill at his house, and I was checking my dummy phone constantly on the way there.

In my opinion, these niggas weren't moving fast enough in finding out who shot at us. Yeah I agreed to let them do their thing, but I recently started doing my own shit too. As we walked into Deshawn's crib, my dummy phone buzzed.

Bit: *Some guys named Jamal, Kevin, and Peter been bragging about it.* *Damn dummies, I thought.*

Me: *Thanks. Get their info; last names and home addresses.*

Bit: *Got it.*

That was my boy Brian. He was an IT major, so he could break into any system and find anyone. His homeboy, Rich was heavy in the streets, so he supplied the names, and then Brian would find their personal info, and then my street soldiers killed.

"Damn nigga, I thought you were a goner," Konz joked as we sat down on the couch.

"I'm sure everybody did. I thank God I'm here though." Deshawn nodded as he stared off.

"Y'all want some juice or pop? I ain't sure of what I got," he asked as he stood up, and Konz and I nodded. Konz lit up a blunt, and inhaled so deeply I thought he was taking the whole thing to the face.

"Damn nigga!" I frowned and he threw me the middle finger.

"So, Kiyuki came and visited me." Deshawn smiled as he re-entered his living room. "Visited me a couple times actually."

"Kiyuki Allen?" I asked to be sure I was hearing right.

"Yes. Looking sexy as hell as usual. She came to see me pretty much the whole last week," he nodded with a smirk.

"How did she get in?" I quizzed.

"Well the first day, she lied and said she was Evelyn, but after that I let them know to put her name on the list for me," he chuckled.

"She pretended to be Evelyn? She's crazy as fuck," I laughed.

"Sexy too. You gone hit?" Konz raised a brow.

"Nigga, I'm with Evelyn." Deshawn shook his head at Konz.

"That's your only reason for not fucking with her?" I grinned as I sipped my pop.

"Hell yeah. If I didn't have a girl, I would be knee deep in that pussy as we speak. I know it's good," he replied and stared into the distance as if he was daydreaming about it.

"Evelyn gone kill yo' ass," I half joked.

"So! She ain't got to know D," Konz frowned.

"I fuck with Evelyn heavy, but she's too feisty. There is a sweet spot that she can't seem to find. I don't like that she's always going off or ready to fuck somebody up," Deshawn exhaled.

"So what are you saying?" I inquired.

"I'm just saying I wish she was more like Namiko and her sisters. They're feisty but they still know their place as women," Deshawn replied.

"Yeah, I get it, but maybe she just going through something," I said and Deshawn shook his head no.

"Some bitches are just like that. Always yelling, fighting, and nagging," Konz said as he blew out smoke.

"Regardless of how any woman is, I'll be damned if she acting a fool on me all the fucking time. I ain't that nigga. You better put her ass over your knee. Shit, she may like that shit," I said, and Konz and Deshawn started laughing.

"You crazy bro. But yeah, I'm giving her another chance. If she keeps that shit up, I'm out," Deshawn nodded to himself.

When I got home, I smelled cheeseburgers. My stomach growled as I rushed to the kitchen.

"Just in time," Namiko smiled as she walked the food over to me.

"Let me go get Aniku." She started to walk off but I grabbed her arm.

"Wha-" she tried to say, but I cut her off with a soft kiss.

When I pulled away, she stared into my eyes, so I gave her another one. The kiss got a little heavier, as she caressed the back of my head, while I groped her little round ass.

"Ugh," Aniku commented as she walked in and grabbed a plate to get some food.

I chuckled and pecked Namiko once more before she went to make herself a plate as well.

DESHAWN SINEAD

„Who the fuck is Kiana!" Evelyn shouted as I watched TV.

This is the shit I was telling Maximilian and Konz about. I didn't say anything in response as I shoved a spoonful of Frosted Flakes into my mouth.

"Hello nigga!" she yelled and crouched down into my face.

"Man move!" I turned my lip up as I looked around her. I felt like I never had any fucking peace these days. I'd rather be back in that coma right about now.

"I'm about to call this hoe myself," She said scrolling through my phone.

"Kiana is my fucking cousin, you nutcase!" I frowned and shot up off the couch to take my bowl to the sink. She called the number anyway, and put it on speakerphone as she followed me to the kitchen.

"Hey cuz," MY COUSIN Kiana answered.

"Oh hey, this is Deshawn's girlfriend, Evelyn just calling to say hi," her dumb ass had to say. I walked past her ass and hopped in the shower.

When I got out, she was sitting on my bed waiting for me. "I'm sorry babe. I just saw she text you about coming over and I got pissed," she exhaled heavily.

"Yeah, like always. You stay bitching for no fucking reason. I'm tired of that shit." I frowned up as I looked through my closet for an outfit to put on.

"I know," she replied as she walked around to face me, and removed my towel.

She dropped down to her knees, and began sucking me off good. I ran my fingers through her short curly hair, as I slowly humped her face.

"Shit," I whispered.

One thing that kept me with Evelyn was her magnificent head game. I knew she was feisty from day one, but at the time I thought it was sexy. Now don't get me wrong, I don't want a woman that I can walk all over, but I don't want a woman that acts like a man either. Evelyn didn't respect me as her man in anyway shape or form. She stayed talking to me crazy, and it didn't matter where we were. In public, in private, at black tie events, Evelyn didn't give a fuck. She was so damn combative, and I hated that shit. If I told her ass to go left, she would go right, just because she didn't want me telling her what to do. I shook my head at my thoughts, then was snapped back to reality when I felt my nut rising.

"Uhhhhh," I grunted as I spilled my seeds down her throat.

She stood her sexy, thick ass up, and strutted over to the bed while stripping. Evelyn was a light bright, and thick in all the perfect places. She looked just like them bitches in the videos. She would be perfect if she could get that mouth together.

She laid on the bed on all fours, and played with her pussy for me to see. I smirked as I walked over, and made sure to grab a condom out of the drawer. Evelyn's ass was already crazy; I would hate to see her pregnant. I slid into her, and she was wet as hell like usual. The intimacy was the only thing going good with us these days.

"Fuck Shawn..." she purred as I stroked her slowly.

I cupped her fat ass, and watched it jiggle in my hands. *Got damn!* I stopped pumping and she started throwing it back on cue. I resumed my thrusts and she kept her motions up as well, and soon we were cumming hard and loud.

"Uhhhhuhhhhh!" we both cried out as I held tightly onto her waist.

"Damn," she panted. "That's why I'm crazy about you." She smiled and I bent down to kiss her full lips. I smacked her ass, and shook my head at how massive that shit was. I slid out, flushed the condom, and then washed my dick so I could resume dressing. "Where are you going?" she frowned as I sprayed Axe all over my body.

"I need to get up with Max," I said looking in the mirror. I was a pretty boy, but I was a thug and bitches loved the combination. I ran my tongue over my perfect teeth, and nodded cause they were white as hell just like I liked them to be.

"When are we gonna spend some time?" she pouted.

"We can go somewhere tomorrow," I replied and leaned down to kiss her lips, but she turned away. "Aight man," I exhaled and walked out the door. She was never satisfied.

After chilling with Max and Konz for a couple hours, I decided to go to this strip joint called Purple Fire. I could've gone to Max's club Red Sugar, but I didn't want to be around people I knew. Also, I was sure that word would get back to Evelyn and I didn't feel like blocking any blows tonight.

I walked in and it was busy as hell. Red Sugar had way more business than this place, but it wasn't bad. I paid the waiter for a table to myself, and ordered multiple drinks in advance, with a plate of chicken wings on the side.

"Alright, are y'all muthafuckas ready for the next girl?" the DJ shouted and everybody cheered as I sipped my beer.

"Welcome to the stage, Sweet Dream!" he yelled as the girl strutted out.

She was sexy as hell, and had a nice ass and plump round titties. She wasn't as thick as Evelyn, but I would take it. She had a mask on, that had cat ears coming out of the top, a black sequin bra, and the matching panties. She had on the highest heels I'd ever seen, which accentuated her perfect calves. She grabbed onto the pole, and spun around, as everybody watched her closely. She must've been good because these niggas were acting like they couldn't do anything else but watch.

Came in the right place, if you're looking for trouble honey. Oh you're looking for trouble honey? Well look here. Miguel's "Destinado A Morir" played through the speakers, as she bounced slowly while removing her bra.

My mouth watered at the sight of her perfect nipples. Her light skin tone was perfect under the pink light that shone on the stage. She rubbed her small, perfectly manicured hands down her body, stopping at the sides of her G-string. She slowly removed it, and every nigga in here cheered. It was so loud that I had to cover my ears until the cheering died down. Once her panties were off, my eyes locked onto her perfectly shaven pussy. I licked my lips, and then looked down at my crotch to see how hard my dick was. I could knock on a door with this shit. She squeezed her breasts, and then twirled around the pole again. She bent over, shook her ass, and then dropped into a split, landing on the pile of money before her. I had to admit, she was bad as hell. She was bad enough to make me come here as a routine customer. I hoped she worked the floor because I definitely wanted a private dance. No, I wasn't gone fuck, but I just wanted this shit to myself for a little bit.

She had so much money that other strippers had to help her collect it before she walked off the stage. I waited and waited to see if she would come out. After twenty minutes, I saw her come out from the back. The mask was off, and her long dark hair hung down her beautiful back. I played cool, as she walked by the many niggas tugging on her wrists. When she got close, I couldn't believe my eyes - Kiyuki Allen. I grabbed her wrist more aggressively than the previous niggas, and she frowned up until she recognized me.

"Deshawn, what are you doing here?" she asked looking around.

"Don't worry about it. How much for a private dance?" I asked biting my lip.

"Deshawn you-"

"How much for a private dance baby girl?" I repeated.

"It's two-hundred dollars," she replied.

"Done," I said licking my lips as I eyed her perfect body.

She rolled her eyes, and then led me to the back. I sat down, and she pulled the curtain closed. She walked over and began swaying seductively. I squinted my eyes, because I was way too turned on. She removed her little top, and I had to adjust in my seat. She walked closer, straddled my lap, and then began to grind slowly. I couldn't help myself, so I leaned up and kissed her neck and collarbone very gently. She let a soft moan escape her mouth.

"Can I touch you?" I asked her and she nodded.

I rubbed my hands down her back, and it was the softest thing I'd ever touched. She got off my lap, and removed her panties slowly to the beat of "Practice" by Drake. I pulled her close, and kissed all over her flat stomach, as she ran her soft hands over my curls. I squeezed her plump ass, and then ran a finger across her wet slit.

"I have to go," she said pulling away as soon as the song went off.

"Kiyuki, chill with me for a little bit," I said still in the moment.

"Deshawn, I have to make some more money." She shook her head and put her clothes on.

I nodded and stood up off the couch. I towered over her, and dipped my tongue into her mouth. *What the fuck was I doing?* I sucked the life out of her lips, and she did the same. She finally pulled away, and then rushed out of the room. I paused for a second so that I could allow my dick to go back soft. I walked out after a couple minutes, and surprisingly became angry when I saw Kiyuki entertaining some random. I brushed it off, and then headed home.

"You coming in at 10pm nigga? Really? Max is at home so where the fuck were you?" Evelyn shouted as soon as I got in the door.

"With my brother Robbie," I replied dryly.

"You better not be lying nigga!" she yelled and pushed me into the dresser.

I closed my eyes so I could take a deep breath, then changed into my pajamas. Evelyn and my relationship had run its course, and Kiyuki was looking like the next movement. I dreamed about fucking her sexy Blasian ass all night.

KIYUKI

A COUPLE WEEKS LATER....

Deshawn: *You still coming?*
Me: *I guess, lol.*

I smiled and put my phone down, and then proceeded to lotion my body. Yes, I was going to chill with Deshawn while Evelyn was in class. I didn't give a fuck about her feelings, and honestly it's not my job to. It's on her nigga to stay faithful, not Kiyuki.

I slid my dark pink tube dress over my head, and then slid into some nude sandals. I let my dark, curly hair hang loose today, and adorned my wrists and neck with some gold bangles and a gold necklace. After spraying my perfume, I walked out the door.

"Damn you look good," Deshawn smiled as I stood at his door.

"Thank you," I smirked and walked into his house.

It was much nicer than I expected, but I guess since he worked with Max, he had bread too.

"I made some pasta for lunch," he grinned, flashing his beautiful teeth.

"What? You can cook?" I chuckled as I stood up.

"I can," he nodded and grabbed my hand to lead me to the kitchen.

The pasta smelled so good, but I could tell it was gonna be spicy because it tickled my nose.

"Thank you," I half smiled as he set the plate in front of me, accompanied by some white wine.

"So you know I'm never one to beat around the bush, why do you have me here?" I asked as I twirled my fork in the pasta.

"Cause I like being around you," he replied.

"What does Evelyn the bulldog think about that?" I inquired and he burst into laughter.

"Why does she have to be a bulldog?" he snickered.

"Because she is! She's always barking and trying to attack," I chuckled.

"True. Well, she has no idea that I have you over here," he shrugged and sipped his wine.

"And I'm guessing she has no idea that you come to Purple Fire every night that I work either," I smirked.

"Hell no she doesn't," he exhaled as if he was frustrated. I smiled and then continued to eat this bomb ass pasta.

After the nice little lunch, we went into the living room to relax.

"Ah," I groaned as I removed my sandals.

"What's wrong?" he asked.

"My feet hurt. I wear heels so much now, that when I wear flats it hurts," I responded.

"Put your foot up here," he said patting his lap. I paused and laughed at his ass. "What? I'm gonna give you a foot massage," he cheesed.

I rolled my eyes playfully, and put my feet into his lap. I sipped my wine, and watched him work his magic. My feet hurt so badly, and his big strong hands felt so good.

"You know if you just want to fuck, all you have to do is ask," I half joked.

I wasn't a bitch that needed to be romanced. No guy ever romanced me; I always had somewhat business relationships. I give up the pussy, and they hand me the cash. I had never been with a person who took me out to dinners, or made love to me.

"Why do you have to be that way? You're too pretty to let shit like that come out of your mouth." He shook his head.

"Because I'm not those girls that need five-star dinners and yacht rides. Just break me off some bread, and I'll break you off with some pussy." I shrugged and took another sip.

"You may not be one of those girls but you should be. I can tell you're wifey material, but you won't let a nigga bring that out of you. You're scared that you'll get done wrong, and be left broken-hearted." He nodded as if he was so sure.

"You don't know anything about me," I scowled while still letting him massage my feet.

"I know enough. You're better than those girls that spread their legs for any nigga that got some bread," he scoffed.

"I don't spread my legs for any man with some bread!" I semi-shouted because I was getting angry.

"Yeah, not anymore." He bit his lip, and tugged me closer to him.

He stared into my eyes and I started to get hot all over. He positioned me so that I was straddling him, and then he pulled me so close I could feel his heartbeat against my chest. For the first time in my life I was speechless. He pecked my lips softly, and I jumped. He chuckled at me, and then went back in. He sucked my lips, and wrestled with my tongue as his hands groped me all over. He trailed from my lips to my neck and collarbone, and it felt so good that I wanted to cry. I was moaning softly and we weren't doing anything but kissing. He kissed my chin, and then pulled my lips back into his mouth. I finally cupped his head and kissed him just as hard as he was kissing me. Suddenly, he pulled away from the kiss.

"That's how you should let a nigga kiss you. I just made love to you without even sliding inside," he said in a low tone as I panted heavily.

Why was I so out of breath? I finally came to, and then climbed off of his lap as he cackled. I put on my sandals, and then stood up to leave.

"Where are you going Kiyuki?" he frowned.

"I have somewhere to be," I lied.

"Don't keep running from me. I'm coming for you." He bit his lip and my pussy throbbed. I just cleared my throat and rushed out.

I didn't like what he did to me. If he could do that to me with just kisses, I could only imagine what the sex was like. No wonder Evelyn acted like a dog with rabies when it came to him. She didn't have to worry though, because I was not gonna be messing with Deshawn's ass. He'd have me so gone, that I'd be handing over my paycheck to his ass.

I sped to Larry's house. While driving, I lightly touched the places Deshawn kissed, because I was still in shock. As soon as I got to Larry's home, I let him fuck me like a hoe on the street to erase the way Deshawn made me feel. I didn't want to be made love to, and most importantly- I didn't want love.

NAMIKO

I was lying in bed stuffing my face on this lazy Saturday morning. I'd finished all my assignments yesterday, so I had all day to relax with my fat self. I wished Max was here too, but he'd been hitting the streets damn near all day.

I heard some rustling downstairs, and I put the TV on mute to make sure that I wasn't tripping. I took a sip of my pop, and then heard the sounds again. I grabbed a pocketknife that I had in the nightstand drawer, and then crept downstairs. This house was huge, but I had hearing like a dog. I heard the sound coming from Max's office, so I smiled assuming that it was him. As I walked down the long hall to approach him, his mother's boyfriend, Alfred slid out in front of me.

"Namiko!" He grinned.

"Mr. Cole? Wh-what are you doing here?" I asked.

"I just came to see how my step daughter-in-law was doing," he smiled.

"Oh, I'm fine. Who's in the office?" I quizzed.

I knew it wasn't Max because he wouldn't dare let this nigga in our home. Before he could answer, Max's mother Gwendolyn walked out of his office.

46

"Ms. Gwen?" I frowned and then looked at Alfred.

"Hey honey! I told you to call me mama," she smiled as she clutched her purse.

"What are you guys doing here? And in Max's office?" I questioned.

"Oh, I was just picking something up from him." She nodded and walked past me with Alfred right behind her.

He made sure to eye my body lustfully before doing so however. Ugh! I followed after them because this was all so confusing. Max hated Alfred and also, he never let anyone go into his office. It was locked while he was gone so I wasn't even sure as to how she got in.

"Ms. Gwen! I mean ma, what-"

"Don't mention this to Maximilian, okay?" she winked and waited for a response.

"I can't just keep this from him. I need to know what you guys are doing here!" I shouted.

"You'll keep it to yourself if you know what's good for you, little fortune cookie," she chuckled and so did Alfred.

I watched as they left the house, then immediately locked the door. I rushed back to Max's office and jiggled the door handle, which was now locked. How the fuck did she get in here? I wobbled around the house, and checked to make sure all the doors were locked securely, before plopping down in the den. I watched TV for a little bit, before drifting off to sleep.

I woke up to the sound of rustling again, so I rushed out to see Max walking through the foyer. He had on light colored jeans, a red crew neck, and red and white Chuck Taylor's.

"Did I wake you, babe?" he smirked and I blushed. I shook my head no, as he approached me and kissed my stomach.

"Are you hungry? I can cook," I said, as I rubbed my hands up under his shirt and crew neck. His abs were rock hard, and I was horny as usual.

"Nah, we can order pizza," he replied and then headed back to his office, which reminded me of his mom.

I followed after him, and then walked into his office with him. I looked around to see if anything looked disheveled, but everything was in place. Max sat down in his chair, and picked up his office phone.

"You want your own pizza again?" he cheesed.

"Yes asshole." I nodded and went to sit in his lap.

I listened as he ordered the food, and then waited until he hung up. He exhaled heavily, and massaged my back as I sat in his lap.

"Max, your mother and Alfred came over today," I said not caring about Gwendolyn's threats.

"Alfred? What the fuck were they doing here?" he frowned his gorgeous face.

"They wouldn't tell me, but your mom was in here," I responded.

"In my office? How?" he asked himself aloud.

I just shrugged because I had no idea either. He pulled his phone from his pocket and dialed his mother. I became nervous because I didn't know what she had planned for me since I told.

"Hey baby!" Gwendolyn sang through the phone.

"Ma, why the fuck you have that weak ass nigga in my crib?" Max yelled.

"I don't know what you're talking about baby," she smiled it sounded like.

"Ma, you know I'm not dumb. You were here, and with that nigga. I want to know why!" he boomed and even I jumped.

"I wasn't over there," she stated matter-of-factly.

"If I find out that Alfred has you on some bullshit, it's gone be a problem and he don't want that with me," Max threatened. Before she could respond he hung up the phone.

"Get the locks changed tomorrow," he told me and I nodded.

We ate the pizza in bed while watching movies, like we'd been doing every Saturday.

"I married my best friend," I said as I bit my fifth slice.

"And to think you wanted to get rid of me at first," he chuckled and wiped the sauce off of my cheeks.

"I'm glad you didn't let me," I smiled with cheeks full of pizza.

"I wasn't letting you go that easily," he replied and sipped his pop. "I worked too hard to get you," he added and we laughed.

"Well, I appreciate your persistence," I said as I stroked his small chin hair.

"I would kiss you but you got sauce all over your face," he laughed.

I swallowed my last bite, and then straddled him slowly. "Namiko, wipe your mouth!" he shouted while giggling.

I leaned down close to him with my lips poked out, as he playfully blocked me. After about one hundred unsuccessful attempts of trying to kiss him with my sauced up face, I climbed off of him and pouted.

"You mad because I won't kiss your messy mug," he chuckled.

I acted as if I didn't hear him, so he climbed on top of me and kissed my lips slowly. He kissed all over my face, despite the pizza sauce. I snickered as he kissed me.

"You a freak for making me do that shit," he grinned.

I smiled and wrapped my legs around his waist, as we continued to kiss passionately.

MAXIMILIAN

Money was missing from my safe the day that I went to pick Deshawn up from the hospital. At first I thought it was Konz stealing, and that he had lied about his hustle, but now I knew exactly who it was - my own damn mother. I installed a camera in my office to see who the culprit was, the day after getting Deshawn, and when I played it back I saw her sneaky ass in my shit.

For one, I was confused as to how she got a key to my office, and secondly, how she knew the combination code to my safe. Because of this little incident, I recently bought a warehouse space, and had safes drilled into the walls. The only person who was gonna know the combo to it was Namiko, in case something happened to me. Anybody else, including Konz was not gonna have that info.

I drove over to see my mother, because I needed answers as to why she was stealing from me. I was pretty sure it was for her nigga, and that infuriated me. I gave my mother money all the time, so she had no reason to take from me for her own gain, which is how I knew this shit was all because of Alfred.

I walked up her walkway, and twisted my face up at how badly manicured the lawn was. I was a neat freak and always liked to have shit perfect. I banged on the door, and pressed the doorbell repeatedly.

I heard whispering and rustling, and I knew it was about to be some shit.

"Open up Ma!" I shouted. The door finally came open, and her hair was all over her head. "Where the fuck he at?" I asked as I barged in and searched through the house.

"Who honey?" she smiled.

"That nigga Alfred! The nigga who got you stealing from your own son!" I yelled.

"I haven't stolen from you Maximilian!" she grimaced.

"Ma, I got you on tape!" I glared at her and she was speechless. "Come out you bitch ass nigga!" I hollered over the house.

"Maxi-"

"I told you he can't be up in here!" I shouted at my mother. Alfred finally crawled his weak ass from the back, staring at me with a smug expression.

"What's up Max?" he smiled.

"Nigga, get yo ass out!" I yelled and pointed towards the door.

"Gwendolyn wants me here," he replied and folded his arms over his burly chest.

"Well if you know what's good for you, you'll get the fuck out." I flared my nostrils and balled my fists up. I was ready to go toe to toe with this nigga. He stared me down before finally rushing out.

"You can't do this Maximilian!" my mother screamed at me.

"I told you what it was from jump. If you want me paying for this crib, he can't be over here. You're free to go to his house," I said plopping down on the couch, and cutting on the television.

"I can't go to his house," she said as she sat next to me.

"Why?" I frowned up preparing for the trifling shit she was about to tell me.

"Because he lost his home. He's living with his sister at the moment." She shook her head. I shook mine as well, and scoffed.

"Ma, you're so much better than that nigga," I exhaled.

"Yet, you still accuse me of stealing. You believe anything your little girlfriend tells you." She turned her lip up in disgust.

"Girlfriend? Really ma? And I have you on camera, I told you that," I said reaching for the Oreos that were sitting on the coffee table.

"I wasn't at your wedding, so she may not even be your wife for all I know," she replied and took a cookie from the package as well.

"Ma, quit that, I can't have you disrespecting my wife," I sighed.

"You disrespect my man!" she shouted.

"Yes, because he disrespects you! I bet you he's living with another woman, he ain't got no fucking sister," I frowned.

"You don't know what you're talking about," she huffed and ran her hand over her hair.

"Why were you stealing my money?" I asked after a couple moments of silence.

"I wanted to help him get an apartment. He needed the deposit money," she responded without looking at me.

"Wow Ma. And you don't see the bad in him? He got you stealing from your own son!"

"I chose to do that, not him!" She glared at me and pointed a finger into her chest.

"And he was right there supporting you, instead of telling you not to do it," I spat and stood up.

"Where are you going?" she looked up at me.

"Home to my wife," I replied.

"Maybe I can come over for dinner, as some sort of peace offering," she half smiled. "I really want to get along with her."

"Bet," I said before leaving.

❧

Tonight, Namiko and I were at The Whitney eating. She was getting bigger and I was becoming very anxious to meet my son.

"Your hair seems longer babe," I said, as I stared at her while at the table.

"I know, but I think it's gonna fall out after he gets here," she smirked.

"Maximilian? This bottle comes from the young man over there," the waiter said setting a bottle of champagne down. There was a note attached, so I pulled it off to read.

You're gonna pay for Pete. Enjoy this as a toast to your last days, it read.

"What's it say?" Namiko asked as I searched the room with my eyes. Finally, they landed on this cat named Cobra, and he smiled and held his glass in the air. "Max." Namiko tried to get my attention.

"I'll be right back Nami," I said as I got up and walked outside. A couple seconds later, Cobra came outside.

"What the fuck is this?" I frowned and threw the note at him.

"You set my brother up," he smiled.

"I already told yo' ass that someone else killed and robbed him," I said through gritted teeth, as random people walked by.

"Well, we need the product that we planned to get." He folded his arms.

"I need the money. I'm not giving away any fucking freebies. Maybe your brother should've been strapped," I spat and he grabbed my collar. I shoved him back so hard, he fell onto the ground. "Don't you ever touch me muthafucka! You're beneath a nigga like me and you need to remember that! If you want the product, send the money! If not, keep it pushing!" I towered over him.

"This ain't fair Maximilian. My brother was killed and I know you had something to do with it," he panted as he stood up off the ground.

"Believe what you want. If you send another threat, you'll be joining your brother, and this time it will be because of me." I shoved him again, and he fell onto the hood of someone's car.

I stormed back into the restaurant and dropped $200 on the table before grabbing Namiko.

"What was that bottle for?" she asked.

"Nami, stop asking questions. If I want you to know something, I will tell you," I whispered in her ear as we walked out.

"Beautiful girl Maximilian." Cobra winked as he passed us to go back inside.

I opened my car door for Namiko, and stopped her before she got in.

"I didn't mean to be rude baby, but it's better the less you know," I said and kissed her lips.

"I know," she replied and caressed my face.

Times were already crazy, and shit was about to get crazier.

KIYUKI

After another long night at Purple Fire, I was extremely exhausted. My life seemed to continue on a downward spiral. Namiko was still kind of cold towards me, but I was happy that she had no idea I was behind all the shit that happened to her, because that would only make things worse. I missed my relationship with her and I knew that information would ruin us for good. I'd tried avoiding Deshawn, but that didn't work. For some reason, I still thought about him all the damn time. Then there was Larry, who was becoming more and more annoying, and even more scared of Max. He told me they caught three of the four guys we hired, and since none of them told they were murdered. They were still looking for the fourth dude, a guy named Chris. I had the perfect plan to make sure if anybody went down, it wouldn't be me.

As I was unlocking my front door, I heard footsteps behind me. I quickly turned around, and let out a sigh of relief when I saw it was Deshawn. I pushed my door open, and then took my key out of the knob.

"Deshawn-" before I could finish, his tongue was down my throat.

We kissed hungrily, and he slammed and locked the front door behind him. We stripped out of our clothes, as we headed to my bedroom. He lightly pushed me onto the bed, and took my panties off swiftly. He tugged me to the edge of the bed, and started to suck my clit.

"Ahhh, shit," I moaned as he sucked, licked, and slurped. He worked his tongue into all the crevices and right places. "Deshaawwnnnn," I cried out as I gripped the sheets.

I tried to back away after cumming for the second time, but he wouldn't let up. I laid there defeated, as he feasted between my legs, making me nut time after time. He spread my legs wider, and licked slowly while admiring the sight.

"I knew this shit tasted good," he said in between licks. I sat there trembling as I watched him continue to slowly suck on my clit, and then lick between the slit slowly.

"Deshawn, please babe," I begged. I'd never came this hard from head.

He stood up, and his long, thick dick stared me down. I never thought a pretty boy could have a dick like this. I opened my mouth, and leaned towards it to suck it, but he stopped me.

"Tonight's about you. I'm gonna make love to you cause that's what you need," he said in a serious tone. I simply nodded as he laid me back down. He climbed in between my legs, and I stopped him by touching his pelvis. "Relax. I'm gonna wear a cap." He smiled and started to kiss my neck while fingering me.

He kissed down to my nipples and sucked them gently, while plunging his fingers into me at a faster pace.

"Ahhhh oh my gosh!" I purred.

Why was he doing all of this to me? He sat up and quickly rolled down a condom, then placed my legs over his forearms. He rubbed his hard dick against my wet pussy, and I pushed myself towards it, only for him to move away.

"I'm in control," he reminded me and I nodded.

He slowly penetrated me, and because I'd only been fucking small ass Larry, it hurt. He slowly went in and out of me, as I made all kinds of faces. He dropped down closer to me, and pinned my hands above my head, as he stroked me very slowly, but extremely good. He rotated his hips, and slammed into me every now and then, hitting my spot like no other. He stared down into my face for a bit, before taking my lips into his mouth. I came so hard, as we tongued each other down.

"Look how that pussy is responding," he smirked. "Every girl needs this Yuki," he whispered, as he began to kiss me again. It was a wrap; this nigga had me gone. "Fuck," he grunted as he kept his strokes nice and slow. "I want this pussy to be mine," he moaned.

"What-what about Evelyn?" I panted as I felt another damn orgasm rising.

"Not a factor," he responded and dipped his tongue back into my mouth.

He fucked me, or made love to me, all damn night. Evelyn blew up his phone but he cut it off, so we could make love in peace.

When I woke up, he made me breakfast and I was happy to know he didn't just dip. "So what now?" I chuckled as we laid back in bed.

"You keep your legs closed to any nigga that ain't me," he replied sternly.

"Deshawn, I'm not gonna be your loyal side chick," I huffed.

"You're too good for that," he said as he kissed the back of my hand.

"You're gonna break up with Evelyn?" I inquired.

"I am," he said as he crawled back between my legs. I smiled and helped him remove my nightshirt.

NAMIKO

ax's mother was gonna eat dinner with us tonight. He said that it was her way of making peace after threatening me. I hoped she was being honest, because I wasn't trying to have beef with my mother-in-law.

Her favorite meal was chicken fried steak, mashed potatoes and greens, so that's what I was making tonight. I was sweating profusely from making all this food, especially the buttermilk gravy that I had to pour over the steak.

"Hey babe," Max walked in with his mother.

"Hey. Hello Ms. Gwen," I smiled and she gave me a shit-eating grin. *Okay?* I thought. "The food is almost ready, and I made cheese-cake with brown sugar pecan sauce on top," I cheesed.

"I'm allergic to pecans," Gwendolyn half smiled.

"Oh, well I think we have some fudge that I can put over it for you," I offered and she nodded.

"So when can we eat?" Max asked.

"When Aniku gets here," I responded as I stirred the gravy.

"Babe, Aniku is with Konz tonight," Max said.

"What? Why?" I frowned.

"Is there something wrong with my son?" Gwendolyn raised a brow referring to Konz.

"No, of course not," I smiled and resumed cooking. "The food will be done in ten minutes; you guys can go sit down and I will bring drinks," I added, and they both got up and headed to the dining room.

I pulled the passion fruit lemonade that I made from the fridge, and took the pitcher to the table. I poured them both a glass, and then set the glass pitcher at the middle of the table.

"Uh Namiko, honey, I need more ice. This is way too warm," Gwendolyn smiled.

"Sure Ms. Gwen," I nodded and took her glass to add more ice. I brought her drink back, and then went to make the plates.

"Ah! Namiko, this is way too much gravy! Not everyone is a small thing like you!" Max's mother yelped.

"Well there is an extra one in the kitchen, I can bring that and let you put your own gravy on," I replied.

"That'll be great, hurry," she waved me off.

"Ma, don't wave her off like that," Max glared at her.

"I'm sorry honey, I didn't mean it that way," she smirked and I nodded.

After dinner, I grabbed the plates and sliced the cheesecake to put it on the small dessert plates.

"Namiko honey, do you have some aspirin?" Gwendolyn entered the kitchen as I was pouring the brown sugar pecan sauce on Max and my slices.

"Sure, I will be right back," I said and went to get it for her.

"Is this mine?" she asked when I got back, and pointed to the third slice of cheesecake.

"Yes, with the fudge," I cheesed, and she smiled and grabbed it.

I carried Max's and mine to the dining room, and we all started to dig in. I realized mine was fudge, and almost had a heart attack.

"Ah!" Gwendolyn screamed as she grabbed her neck.

"Ms. Gwen, I'm so sorry!" I shot up out of my seat as Max tended to his mother.

"Call 911!" he yelled to me and I did so.

The whole time I placed the call I wondered how this happened. I specifically put hers on the left side so that I'd remember, so how did she get the wrong one?

"Okay, they're coming," I said as I watched Gwendolyn appear to be dying.

"Babe, how did you mix this up?" Max stared up at me with worried eyes.

"I don't know Max, I-I thought I was being careful," I whined because I was just as confused as he.

The ambulance came and rushed her outside. Max followed after her and I tried to come too, but he stopped me. I felt like shit as I went back into the house, and cleaned the plates up. Maybe the baby was messing with my memory, but I know that I had them set up in a certain order. I shook my head as I cleaned the dining room and kitchen, then retired upstairs.

As I was lying in bed, I heard Aniku walk by. I rushed outside of my bedroom and stopped her.

"Why are you hanging out with Konz?" I folded my arms. I was starting to feel like Kiyuki.

"He's just my friend Nami," she smiled.

"Promise?" I raised a brow and she nodded and laughed.

"Okay, goodnight," I smirked.

I heard the front door open around 1am, and I sat up to wait for Max. He walked into the room, and I could tell he was exhausted.

"How is she?" I whispered.

"She's fine now. She thinks you tried to kill her," he exhaled.

"What? Why would I do that?" I frowned and turned the light on.

"Turn that back off Nami. And what do you expect? She specifically told you that she was allergic to pecans and somehow she gets the pecan sauce by mistake?" He shook his head.

"You think I purposely gave her that sauce Max?" I quizzed.

"Nah babe, I don't. I hope you didn't. I just want you to understand where she's coming from," he said as he stripped down to nothing. He walked over to the dresser, and threw on some pajama sweats before getting in bed.

"Are you mad at me?" I finally asked.

"No, I know it was an accident." He kissed my lips and palmed my belly.

"Dinner was real good by the way. It wasn't too much sauce, it was perfect," he added and I blushed.

"I'm glad you liked it," I smiled as he kissed me gently.

"I love you, Namiko," he whispered.

"I love you too, Maximilian," I whispered back, as he removed my shirt.

MAXIMILIAN

I sat outside this nigga Jamal's house, preparing myself. I knew he was one of the niggas bragging about shooting at Deshawn and I, so I was gonna take his bitch ass out. Two other guys, Kevin and Peter, Deshawn and I killed already, so we just needed to off Jamal and this nigga named Chris that we couldn't seem to find. Chris was the one we really wanted, because he was the one hired. From that point he recruited Jamal, Kevin, and Peter, so those three had no idea who wanted us dead, but Chris did.

I put my blunt out, and then made sure my silencer was on, on my gun. I wanted to make this shit quick and easy. I pulled my hoodie on and walked up his walkway. He was sitting on his porch smoking a blunt with a friend, like he didn't have a care in the world.

"Can I help you?" He squinted his eyes as he tried to see who I was.

I simply pulled my gun from my waist, and shot he and his friend between the eyes. Once they slumped over, I turned right back around without saying a word; three down, and one more muthafucka to go.

After taking that muthafucka out, I started wondering if Cobra was gonna make good on the threat he'd sent my way. I wasn't in the mood to be entertaining two wars at once, but I would if need be.

When I got home, it was around 2am, and I heard Aniku on the phone with my little brother. I didn't know what his plans were with her, but I didn't need his dumb ass decisions fucking up what I had with my wife.

I walked upstairs and headed straight to the shower, to clean off the day's grime. Once I came out, I saw Namiko on the bed examining her protruding belly.

"What are you doing?" I chuckled.

"Wondering how much bigger this is gonna get," she frowned.

"At 2am? I don't think it's good for you to be up this late when you're pregnant, babe." I shook my head.

"I know but I wanted to wait for you," she smiled. I walked over to the bed, and cut the lamp off before climbing in.

"Thank you, but the shit I do calls for late hours, so you should get your sleep Nami," I said, kissing her hand. I palmed her belly with both of my hands as we stared at each other.

"Just three more months," she whispered.

"I know. Then we will officially be parents," I said in a low tone. I bent down and started kissing her belly, and then removed her panties.

"Max, what are you doing?" she moaned. I kissed her lower lips softly, and then put my finger inside her. "Ahhh," she cooed. I put her legs on my shoulders, and then began to make love to her with my mouth. She tasted so good, and I went at it for forever until she begged me to stop. "Maxx..." she whimpered. I licked her one last time, and then kissed her belly again.

"Soon as he comes out, I'm putting another one in," I said more so to myself.

"No, especially because we're having a natural birth. I'm gonna need a break," she giggled.

"Aight you brat," I joked, and she turned her back to me. She reached for my hand, and brought it around to touch her stomach.

The next morning, I showered and brushed my teeth around 9am so I could go to the gym. My legs and arms still felt stiff sometimes, so the doctor recommended that I do some gym exercises. I used to live in the gym, but that slowed down once I got married and shit. As I was doing some leg weight lifts, I heard a familiar voice call my name.

"Melissa? What's up?" I panted.

"Nothing, just working out like you," she cheesed. She had on the shortest, tightest shorts, and a tight ass sports bra that her nipples poked through.

"I see," I said clearing my throat.

"So how is your wife?" she asked.

"Perfect like always," I nodded.

"Good. I see you needed that physical therapy," she gestured towards the machine.

"Yeah, some parts get a little stiff sometimes," I replied.

"So are you gonna be here much longer? Maybe we can have some breakfast," she offered.

"I'm not leaving for another two hours," I said.

"Well lunch?" she grinned.

"Melissa, that's not really appropriate." I shook my head frowning.

"Having lunch with a friend?" she cocked her head in confusion.

"A female friend in particular. I wouldn't want my wife having lunch with any man but me, so I need to do the same," I responded dabbing the sweat off my face.

"Well, there's no harm in us working out together," she chuckled and sat at the machine next to me.

"You're not gonna leave even if I ask you to, huh?" I quizzed and she shook her head no. I shook my head at her, and then resumed my exercise.

"So how long have you been married?" she asked.

"We've been together almost seven years, and married for three," I lied. See, these hoes always asked that to see if they had a chance or not. In their minds, the lower the number, the better chance they had in snagging you. I wouldn't dare tell her Namiko and I have only been married about ten months.

"Wow. Nice," she replied as she stared off into abyss. I laughed inside because my plan worked. "That's a long time," she added.

"Yeah, and I've enjoyed every moment," I nodded.

"I bet. Especially when I caught you two having sex in the hospital," she reminded me and I laughed.

"Oh yeah, the thought of getting caught made it better," I chuckled at the memory.

"Your smile is so sexy." She bit her lip.

"Thank you," I half smiled.

"You're just sexy period." She licked her lips.

"If you're gonna work out with me, I need you to be quiet," I replied sternly.

"Yes sir," she smiled and we continued to work out in silence, thank God.

DESHAWN

"You're not going out again!" Evelyn shouted as she followed me through the house. I ignored her ass just like usual, and continued to look for my shoes. "I'm coming with you," she added and ran to the room to get dressed.

I quickly put on the shoes closest to me, and then jogged out to my car. I sped off, and ten minutes later, she was blowing up my phone. I chuckled to myself, as I thought about what I'd just done. Yesterday evening, I'd taken Kiyuki out to the mall, and then we went to see a movie. I was really feeling her, and to her knowledge, Evelyn and I were done. Only thing saving me was the fact that she and Namiko were estranged, so she had no sources to tell her I was still fucking with Evelyn.

I didn't want to be with Ev anymore, but I was never one to make rash decisions. I needed to make sure I was choosing the right one. Kiyuki may feel like the right one now, but she may end up being a nagging ass burden like Evelyn in the end.

I exhaled heavily when I saw Evelyn hadn't let up on calling me. I put my shit on silent *and* do not disturb so that I wouldn't even hear that shit. I pulled up to Kiyuki's crib, and grabbed the movies I'd brought from the back seat. I had to put them in my car prior, while

Evelyn was in class, because otherwise she would've been even more down my back.

"Hey daddy," Kiyuki greeted me and kissed my lips.

See this is what a nigga wanted to come home to, not a damn war. Kiyuki was that down ass bitch, that let a nigga be a man. When I say be a man, I don't mean cheating and shit, I mean be the provider, and make decisions that were in both of our best interests. She didn't challenge every word that came out of my mouth, and she was the perfect amount of feisty.

"What did you bring?" She smiled looking beautiful as ever.

I'd made her quit that strip club, because I didn't want everybody seeing my girl. I offered to fund her lifestyle, while she worked on drawing. She said she wanted to create cartoons one day, but she was too embarrassed to tell people that. I thought it was dope and cute.

"I brought *Roots*," I joked.

"Umm, okay. How long is that?" she cheesed.

"Like six hours." I nodded and she turned her lip up. "I'm fucking with you," I chuckled, and so did she.

As we watched the movie, I couldn't keep my eyes off of her. She had on boxer shorts, a tight t-shirt, and her hair was down.

"Come here," I said as I pulled her close. I sniffed her semi-wet hair, and got a whiff of lavender.

"Deshawn, who knows that we're together?" she asked out of nowhere.

"Maximilian, Konz, and my little brother," I replied honestly.

"Not Evelyn?" she inquired further.

"Not yet, but she will," I said and shook my head. I knew after a couple more dates, word would get back to Evelyn that someone saw us together.

"I better not find out I'm on the side, or even a main. I better be the only one," she responded.

"You are," I half lied.

At this point, it felt like Evelyn was the side chick and Kiyuki was the main. Most nights I slept over Kiyuki's and told Evelyn some bullshit when I got back home around noon.

"Good," she smiled and I admired her beauty.

Even in the dark, how gorgeous she was, was very apparent; from her smooth vanilla skin tone, to her beautiful slanted honey eyes. She cupped my face, and I dipped my tongue into her mouth.

"Come on." I said as I led her to the bedroom. I was about to eat that pussy from the back all night.

❧

"All right babe, I'll be back around six after I put in some work with Maximilian," I told Kiyuki as I headed to my crib. "I have a surprise for you," I winked and she blushed.

I drove home, and mentally prepared myself for what was to come. I couldn't remember if Evelyn had a morning class today or not, but I hoped she did. I pulled up and saw her outside, along with some of my clothes all over the lawn. I hopped out the car, and jogged inside to hear "Give a Chick a Hand" by Mya, blasting throughout the house.

"Evelyn!" I shouted as I made my way to the back bedroom.

When I walked in, Evelyn was snatching my shit off the hangers and singing the song word for word. "I'ma give a chick a hand, walk up to her shake her hand, I'ma give a chick a hand, I'ma give a chick a hand, I'ma be a good sport, walk up to her, shake her hand. She took my man she did, she took my man she did. I don't know how she did though, cause I'm a bad chick so, I'ma give a chick a hand," she sang along loudly. I cut the music off, and she turned around to look at me.

"Get out!" she shouted.

"This is my fuckin' crib! You get the fuck out," I frowned and grabbed the stuff I needed to take a shower. As I walked to the bathroom, Evelyn started raining blows on my back.

"I know you're fucking Kiyuki nigga!" she screamed as her small fists pounded me.

I ignored her and turned the water knobs in the shower. She kicked me in the ass, and I hit my head on the shower wall before falling into the tub and getting soaked. I hopped out of the tub, and she booked it to the bedroom with me hot on her heels. I grabbed her and pinned her to the wall, as she panted.

"It's over Evelyn. Yes, I'm fucking somebody else. Our shit has run its course. I'm done," I said through gritted teeth as water dripped from the tip of my nose.

I let her go and she pushed me.

"Fine nigga! Fuck you! That's why I'm gone fuck one of your home-boys, or maybe Robbie!" she laughed and headed to the front door.

"Go ahead and fuck whomever you want, I ain't tripping," I lied.

I would be salty if she fucked my little brother Robbie, but I had to choose between she and Kiyuki. This was sooner than I had liked, but oh well. I took my shower as I felt like a weight had been lifted off my shoulders.

NAMIKO

I couldn't believe that Max's mother thought I'd tried to kill her. I mean I really had no explanation as to why I had accidentally given her the wrong cheesecake. All I kept saying was that I thought I was careful. Aniku says she believes that Ms. Gwen switched it herself, but why would she do that? Why would she put her own life in danger to get back at me? That makes absolutely no sense, unless she's beyond crazy.

I'd baked some lemon bars, and I was gonna take them over to her as some sort of peace offering. She probably wouldn't eat them, but it was the thought that counted, right?

I took a deep breath, and then grabbed my pan out of the car. It was getting harder and harder to lug around this belly, my purse, and anything extra. I couldn't wait to get this boy out of me.

"Well hello, Ms. Namiko," Gwendolyn answered the door.

"Good afternoon Ms. Gwen, I brought these for you," I grinned and reached them out to her. She stared down at them, scoffed, and then walked away from the door. I pulled the pan back close to me, and then walked into her home. "Should I put these in the kitchen?" I smiled.

"Yeah, back in your kitchen. Why would I eat that?" she frowned.

"You don't like lemon?" I laughed nervously trying to lighten the moment.

She rolled her eyes, and turned up the volume on the Maury show. I took the pan to the kitchen anyway, and then came back out to sit on the couch with her.

"Can you not plop down! Don't shake up my grandchild!" she shouted in my ear.

"I'm sorry. I sit like this all the time," I half smiled.

"Well stop, because if my first grandbaby comes out with a problem, you and I are gonna have a problem," she grimaced.

"Uh, okay," I nodded quickly and she fake smiled.

"Now, when is he coming?" she asked.

"April fifth." I looked down at my belly.

"An Aries. That's gonna be an evil child." She shook her head and bit a cracker.

"Why is that?" I inquired.

"Fire sign. They're all evil," she replied without taking her eyes off of the Maury show.

"Maximilian is a Sagittarius," I added and she ignored me.

I guess because I put an end to her fire sign theory, she declined to respond. It was silent for a bit, as I glanced over at her periodically. The only thing that could be heard was the sound of her munching on those crackers, and the women on TV yelling that they were one thousand percent sure some nigga was the daddy.

"So Ms. Gwen, I wanted to apologize for mixing our cheesecake slices up. I thought I was being careful, but I guess when I went to get the aspirin I got mixed up. It must be the baby," I smirked.

"So now it's my damn fault that you tried to kill me?" she questioned and made a face as if she was offended.

"No! No, it's mine. I'm just telling you why it happened. I got thrown off," I pleaded.

"Thrown off by me?" she raised a brow.

"No, thrown off by- look, I'm sorry okay?" I exhaled.

"Right," she said as she munched on a cracker.

"Can I have one?" I asked. I really didn't want to ask her, but I was hungry all the time. She stared me down, rolled her eyes, and then put the package in my face so I could grab one. "Why don't you like me?" I inquired as I bit into the cracker.

"Because you tried to kill me," she responded dryly.

"I didn't- before that Ms. Gwen. You didn't like me before that whole thing happened," I said.

"Just say it," she exhaled.

"Say what?" I frowned.

"That you tried to kill me. Stop saying *that thing*," she turned her lip up.

"Anyway, you didn't like me beforehand." I ignored her comment.

"Before what?" she smirked.

"Before we all had dinner together," I huffed.

"Which dinner?" she chuckled. Fine, I was gonna give her what she wanted.

"The dinner I tried to kill you at," I replied.

"Oh that one. I didn't like you before that because you run your mouth too damn much. You don't need to tell my son everything," she said sipping her water.

"Yes I do. I'm his wife," I responded.

"Oh, I forgot you Chinese people are obsessed with honor and loyalty. You'll learn later in life to keep some things to yourself, just like he keeps things from you." She looked at me and raised a brow.

"Ms. Gwen, for one, I'm half Japanese. Secondly, he doesn't keep anything from me unless it's to protect me."

"Japanese, Chinese, so what," she scoffed.

"Well your grandson will be 75% black, and 25% Japanese so you should want to know what he is," I spat.

"Girl, you look like a black chick. Only thing about you that's Japanese are those eyes, so my grandson won't look too Japanese," she shrugged and smiled.

"I have no problem looking like a black chick since I am one." I shook my head.

"Good, now get off your high horse," she spat and shoved a cracker into her mouth.

"Where is the bathroom?" I rolled my eyes since she was staring at the TV.

"Back there," she pointed to nowhere in particular.

I took a deep breath, and then headed to the back to hunt for a bathroom. I relieved myself, and then got up to wash my hands. All of a sudden, Gwendolyn's boyfriend Alfred burst in.

"Excuse me!" I shouted. He smirked, and then locked the door behind himself.

"How are you?" he smiled and folded his arms.

"I'm fine Alfred, now let me out," I frowned.

"Let's talk for a bit," he said as he neared me.

"About what?" my voice trembled.

He got behind me and caressed my stomach, while his hard dick pressed against my ass. I tried to move, but this old nigga was way stronger than he looked.

"Alfred please, Max is gonna kill you," I whined as he rubbed his hand up my dress.

He ignored me and inhaled my perfume as he ripped my panties off. He let me go, and then licked the crotch of my underwear which were clutched in his big hands. He sucked on the crotch part, as I ran past him and out the bathroom door.

"Ms. Gwen! Alfred is not supposed to be here! And he just ripped my underwear off!" I cried.

"Girl, what are you talking about?" she chuckled and stood up.

"Honey, she's lying," Alfred cackled as he walked out empty handed.

"Wait until I tell Max," I said as I rushed to the couch to grab my purse and leave.

"You're not saying shit!" Gwendolyn shouted as she charged towards me.

All I thought about was her harming my baby, so I swung my heavy bag, knocking the wind out of her. She stumbled backwards, and hit her ass on the hardwood floors.

"Arrggghhhhh!" she called out in pain.

I ran out of the house and sped home, because I didn't know what to do. I was defending my baby and myself! I pulled over after a couple minutes so that I could calm down so I wouldn't go into an early labor. My phone started ringing, and I saw it was Maximilian, so I didn't answer. I immediately called Evelyn, because I needed somewhere to go for now. There was no way I could go home at the moment. I sped to her home, and got there in less than ten minutes.

"What happened?" Evelyn asked frantically.

"Alfred felt me up, and then when I told Gwendolyn she wouldn't listen. When I threatened to tell Max, she charged me and I hit her in the stomach with my purse," I panted.

"You hit her old ass with this big ass shit?" Evelyn burst into laughter as she pointed to my purse.

"Yes! And she flew back onto the hardwood floor. I think she bruised her butt bone," I replied, as Evelyn laughed so hard a tear came out.

"Oh my gosh bitch! You about to kill me," she said out of breath.

"This is not funny Ev! This is my husband's mother!" I squealed trying not to laugh.

"Okay, okay. Look, just tell Max what happened and he should understand. If not, hit his ass with this purse too!" she cracked.

"I hate you," I said shaking my head and chuckling.

🙂

I WALKED INTO THE HOUSE AROUND 8PM, AND I HEARD TUPAC blasting from the gym room. I slowly walked towards it, and saw Max doing some ab exercises. For some reason, he didn't want to go to a public gym anymore.

I entered slowly, and stood there until he saw me. He cut the music off with the remote, and stood his fine ass up. Sweat covered his dark caramel physique, and his muscles seemed to be flexing for me.

"Where have you been?" he asked and sipped his Gatorade.

"With Evelyn," I replied shyly.

"Why you do my mom like that?" he grinned. I couldn't help but laugh and so did he.

"She charged me Max. I'm sorry," I pouted to get his sympathy.

He pecked my lips, and squeezed my butt. I told him what happened and he just shook his head the whole time. I showed him that my underwear was gone, and he immediately got up and stormed out.

"Where are you goi-" I couldn't get it out before the door slammed.

Twenty minutes later, Ms. Gwen called me screaming, as I listened to Maximilian fuck Alfred up in the background.

"I told you to keep your mouth shut you little bitch! You already broke my tailbone!" she shouted and I bucked my eyes. Suddenly the line went dead, and I promptly called Max six times with no answer. Thirty minutes later, he was back and had blood specks on his workout top.

"You killed him?" I asked worried.

"No, just stomped a mud puddle in his ass," he replied as he undressed to shower.

"I broke your mom's tailbone?" I quizzed.

"No, she's bruised up pretty bad back there though. The doctor ordered her to sit on ice." He snickered and went to shower.

For some reason I felt like this was only the beginning of that drama queen Gwendolyn and I.

KIYUKI

I was looking through the arts and crafts aisle of Target, because I wanted to get a new book to sketch in. As I was putting a couple things into my basket, I heard a familiar voice call me a slut. I looked over and saw Evelyn walking down the aisle with her arms folded.

"Can I help you?" I quizzed as I looked at the pencils.

"No, but you can stop helping yourself to my nigga," she frowned.

"Who is your nigga?" I chuckled.

"Deshawn bitch! The same nigga you been fucking every night!" she yelled, making this older man rush off the aisle.

"Yep, every night so that should tell you whose nigga he is." I raised a brow and she ran towards me.

She wrapped her hands around my neck, as we bumped into the shelves and racks. Stuff was flying onto the floor as we tussled with one another. I pushed her backwards, and then put my hand basket onto the floor.

"I been waiting to beat your ass bitch and you just gave me a reason." I flared my nostrils and ran up on her.

I delivered punch after punch as she unsuccessfully tried to block me. We had an audience and I knew this news would be all throughout

Detroit in no time. Once she dropped to the floor, I kicked her in the stomach, and grabbed my basket to leave. Security ran over, as I slipped through the crowd. I heard them asking where the other person was, as I rushed to the line so I could purchase my stuff quickly.

As I was getting my receipt, ambulance sirens became loud as hell. I ran outside and sat in my car, because I wanted to see all the damage I'd caused. I didn't think I'd hurt her that bad, but maybe I did. After awhile, they rushed Evelyn out and she was screaming all types of obscenities at the top of her lungs.

"That bitch is alright," I scoffed and cranked my car to leave. On my way home, Larry called me. I ignored the first call but he called me again right after.

"What?" I spat into the phone.

"Come through, we need to talk," he barked.

"Aight," I huffed and hit the end button.

I pulled up to his house and rolled my eyes as I walked up the porch steps. I saw a roach run by, and wanted to throw up. I rang the doorbell, and the door flung open before the sound finished playing out. As soon as I walked in, Larry grabbed me by the throat and slammed me into the wall.

"Where the fuck have you been bitch?" he shouted, and spit flew everywhere. I shoved him away, and then felt up my sore neck.

"What the hell is wrong with you Lawrence?" I yelled.

"I know you fucking the homie," he glared at me.

"I don't think he's your homie," I chuckled as I sat my Birkin bag on his table.

"And he won't be your fuck buddy anymore once I tell him and Max what you did," he snickered.

"What *I* did?" I pointed to my chest.

"Yeah you!" he laughed. "Unless you stop fucking with Deshawn!" he added.

"Wouldn't it make more sense to fuck with him?" I frowned.

"Yeah, if you weren't feeling his ass! What are you trying, to marry this nigga?" Larry sounded as if he was about to cry.

"Look, calm down. Ain't like you and I were exclusive," I replied.

"Since when? Everybody knows you're mine!" he hollered, and then plopped down on the couch.

"Well not anymore," I responded dryly as I picked my purse back up.

"Is this what you called me over for? I'm a busy woman," I said.

"Yuki, if you keep fucking him, I'm throwing you under the bus," Larry threatened.

"Maybe I should throw you under the bus!" I shouted.

"Who do you think they're gone believe? Their friend, or a skeezer known for lying and scheming?" Larry raised a brow. "Huh?" he added.

"Fine," I finally said.

"Good." He smirked and pulled me close. He rubbed his hands all over my ass, and squeezed hard.

"I want some pussy, come on," he added as he led me to his room.

"I got a yeast infection," I lied.

"Either I get some pussy, or you sucking this dick." He shrugged as he released his dick.

I reached in my purse and threw a condom at him and he grinned. After he rolled it down, I straddled him and started to bounce.

"Shit," he moaned as I rolled my eyes. He tried to get his mouth on my nipple but could barely move as I worked my pussy around his small dick.

"Slow down! Ah-nigga finna nu-nut," he stuttered. I ignored his pleas, and worked him even faster. "Ahhhhhhh! Fuckkkkkkk!" he cried out as he filled up the condom. I hopped off him, grabbed and put on my panties, then headed out.

I needed to do something quick, because I couldn't believe I just cheated on my nigga. I cheated in order to prevent him from finding out that I set up he and his best friend. My life couldn't have been any worse right now.

As I was walking to my car, my phone buzzed and I saw it was a text from Cori's ass. I usually would've ignored it, but she had disappeared so I was interested. I unlocked my phone, and then went to the text.

Cori: *Wait until Namiko and my brother find out what you did to them.*

Me: *No idea what you're talking about.*

Cori: *Play dumb now bitch, but I'm coming for you.*

I rolled my eyes and threw my phone into my purse. That bitch had no proof of what I had done to Namiko and Deshawn, so she was the least of my fucking worries. Hopefully, when she did show her face, Max killed her ass.

I sped home, and quickly showered before Deshawn arrived. I didn't want him knowing I fucked someone else. Could he tell? I mean Larry could never tell, but then again Deshawn had brains. I poured some vinegar into my bathwater, in hopes of tightening my pussy muscles despite Larry's small size. After Deshawn and my date, I was too nervous so I told him I was menstruating. Lord please help me.

MAXIMILIAN

Red Sugar was jumping tonight, and I was proud. I loved to see money coming in. I smiled and bobbed my head, as I watched niggas spend money on everything that we had to offer.

I walked over to the bar, and ordered a double shot of Patrón so that I could go back up and work some more.

POW!

POW!

Gunshots rang out, and everyone scattered about. People were running over one another as they tried to make their way to the front and emergency exits. I searched the place frantically with my eyes, trying to figure out who the culprit was, but I saw nothing or no one. I rushed outside with everyone else, and still no one was there. Once the club was cleared out, I walked back in and saw the lights on the ceiling were busted, as well as a couple speakers. Although not much damage, I was pissed.

"Here boss." The doorman handed me a note.

This is just the beginning. - Cobra. It read. I balled it up, threw it away, and then started to walk out to my car.

"Close down?" Gordon, the manager asked.

"Yes nigga!" I shouted at his stupid ass and left.

I went home, got dressed, and then called Deshawn. This nigga Cobra wanted to play, then we were gonna play. I know he didn't know that I knew where he lived, but unfortunately for him I did. I had the information on all the niggas I supplied product to. I was gonna hit this nigga where it hurts, because I knew right now I couldn't get to him physically.

"So what's the plan?" Deshawn asked as he climbed into the car.

"Going to get this nigga's peoples," I replied and he nodded.

We sped to his mom's crib in Dearborn, and parked a little way's down. It was nighttime, and no one was outside which was perfect. I ran up to the door, and knocked like I was the fucking police. Cobra's mother answered the door, and Deshawn and I barged in.

"Oh! What is going on?" his mother shouted.

His sexy ass sister, Esmeralda ran from the back to see what was going on, so Deshawn snatched her up. I only knew who she was because I ran into her in the club one night, and was fucking on her for a couple of weeks. Cobra never knew that though.

"If you scream, I will blow your brains out. If you cooperate, you'll live," I said as I pressed the cold metal of my .9 mm to his mother's head. She nodded and so did Esmeralda, so we headed to the car.

Deshawn and I blindfolded them, and then sped to the warehouse, because we didn't want them to have any idea as to where they were when we got there.

"Please mister!" Cobra's mother begged as we tied them up in a room in the warehouse. I didn't say anything and neither did Deshawn.

"Please papi!" Esmeralda cried out but seductively.

"Shut the fuck up!" I spat.

We taped their mouths back up, and then sat and waited for Cobra to realize what we'd done. My dummy phone rang, and I saw his number flash across.

"Speak."

"Bring my family back!" he demanded as if he I was scared of him.

"Nah, you done fucked up homie. I don't know who you thought you was fucking with." I chuckled as Esmeralda stared me down.

"What do you want? Money?" he huffed.

"Nah, you. It's either you, or your mother and sister," I spat.

"Fuck!" Cobra shouted.

"This can all go away, if you just give me some product," he replied.

"Nah, you don't have the option to work with me anymore."

"All because I had someone shoot up your little club?" he hollered.

"Do you know how much shit I'm gonna have to go through in order to get people back into my shit?" I frowned. "People ain't gon' wanna come into a spot that got shot up. Detroit is dangerous enough!" I yelled.

"Fine Max. You want to take it to the extreme, we can do that," he said in his thick Spanish accent.

"I ain't worried player," I smirked. The line went dead, and I stood up.

"Goodnight ladies," I said and turned my back.

"Somebody will be here to feed y'all in the morning," Deshawn said to them.

"Don't think about trying to scream through the tape, the room is sound proof," I winked, and we walked outside.

"What are we gone do with them?" Deshawn asked as we headed to his house.

"Keep them for two weeks' tops. If he doesn't show his face before then, we gon' have to figure something out. I don't want to kill his people, but if he pushes me I will," I replied.

"Especially not that sister of his, that's a sexy ass bitch right there," Deshawn chuckled.

"Speaking of women, so you and Kiyuki are official?" I quizzed because I wanted to know, and because I wanted to change the subject from Esmeralda.

"Most definitely," he nodded and smiled.

"Well if you're happy I'm happy," I smiled. Maybe Kiyuki had changed; shit, I hoped she did. I didn't want my homie fucking with a conniving hoe.

"Thanks my nigga," Deshawn replied as he sparked a blunt.

NAMIKO

"A hhhhh!" I screamed as I sat in the pool of water. I was having my son in the middle of the foyer, and I was in so much pain. This whole natural thing was nothing to play with. "Get him out!" I cried.

"Honey, please relax, it's not time yet," the midwife Shelly said as she looked between my legs. "Almost though," she added.

"Relax babe." Max kissed my forehead and wiped my sweaty hair.

"Please just reach in there and pull him out," I whined. I looked over and Gwendolyn rolled her eyes. She reached into her purse, and then lit a cigarette.

"Ms. Gwen, can you put that out please?" the midwife asked. Gwendolyn ignored her as she took another puff.

"Ma! Put that shit out!" Max boomed. She did as she was told and then stood up to pace the floor.

"Okay, it's time to push hun," Shelly smiled. *Thank God!* I thought.

After five damn pushes, Maximilian Kadeem Davis Jr. was finally here. He was so adorable and had a head full of hair.

"Why is he so light?" Gwendolyn yelped.

"He's gonna darken Ms. Gwen," Shelly responded, as she took him from me and handed him to Max. He stared at him for the longest, as I tried to catch my breath.

Shelly cleaned me up, and then helped me upstairs to the bed to rest. I had to make sure MJ was fine before I could rest peacefully though.

For the next few days, Max helped me a lot since I couldn't move as much. I only tore a little, so Shelly was able to stitch me up herself. Like an idiot, I agreed to allow Ms. Gwen to watch the baby and me. I hoped that she would see that I didn't hate her, and maybe we could bond some more.

"Okay, do you need anything before I go?" Max asked after bringing me a tray of breakfast.

"Don't leave!" I whined.

"Baby, my mother is gonna be here," he smiled.

"She hates me," I replied.

"No she doesn't. She's gonna take care of you, watch." He pecked my lips.

"Okay," I half smiled and started back eating my food.

"See you later." He stood up, and then walked over to MJ's crib. "And see you later as well little man." He smiled down at him for a little bit, and then left.

Halfway through my food, Gwen barged in and snatched the tray.

"I'm still eating," I frowned.

"You can't eat like this anymore, the baby is out," she spat and turned on her heels. I would've chased after her but I didn't have the energy.

I watched TV for a couple hours, and then I got up to take a shower. When I walked out, Gwendolyn was sitting on the bed with a tray of food.

"It's lunch time Namiko," she smiled and stood up.

"I'm not that hungry," I lied.

"It's been hours since you last ate, you should be starved," she replied as she peeled the bed covers back. I walked over to my baby, kissed his cheek, and then climbed into the bed.

"Here you go," she smiled and sat the tray across my lap.

I looked down and it was home made chicken noodle soup, corn-bread, and red Kool-Aid. It looked good, but I was scared to eat it.

"Go on," she said in a chipper tone.

"I uh-"

"Oh, you think I'd try and poison you? I'm offended Namiko," she glared down at me.

"No, I don't think tha-"

"Then eat," she cut me off.

I stirred it slowly, trying to see if I could spot anything suspicious. Everything looked okay, so I took a small spoonful and put it in my mouth. It was really good, and tasted just fine.

"Good right?" she cheesed, and I nodded.

"Finish up," she said, and then left the room.

I ate all the soup and the tasty honey cornbread. I downed the Kool-Aid and was stuffed. Gwendolyn came back, and took my tray.

"Would you like some cookies?" she asked.

"Uh, no, I'm good, I'm gonna breast feed I think," I said and started to get up.

"Oh no, he's fine right now. Lay back down," she stopped me.

"Are you sure?" I asked.

"Yes! Remember Namiko, I have had two kids," she replied and left.

I watched TV for a bit, before I finally drifted off to sleep. I woke up suddenly, due to strong pains shooting through my body.

"Ahhhh!" I screamed.

I got up, and ran to the bathroom to throw up violently. My throw up was regular and then all of a sudden it was red. My stomach felt like it was filled with poison. I looked up, and saw Gwendolyn standing in the bathroom doorway.

"Not feeling well?" she raised a brow.

"Ca-call 911!" I shouted as vomit spilled out of my mouth.

"Ahhhhhhh!" Aniku screamed she witnessed the sight.

"Aniku call 911!" I cried. She pulled out her phone and dialed 911, as Gwendolyn stared down at me with a smirk.

I was rushed to the hospital, and my stomach was pumped. They had to feed MJ because it wasn't safe for me to breastfeed him.

"What did you eat?" the doctor asked once I was in the room.

"Soup," I cried.

"Mrs. Davis, there was arsenic in your stomach," she said. "Did someone cook that for you? And did it have white rice in it?" she asked.

"My mother-in-law, and yes it did," I replied.

"Did anyone else eat it?" she asked.

"I believe she did, and my little sister, too," I nodded.

"Okay, sometimes arsenic can be found in the water we drink, especially here in America, as well as white rice. You probably just drank a contaminated batch of water over a long period of time or ate contaminated rice. You will be perfectly fine Mrs. Davis, just try to drink natural bottled water for now and eat brown rice. The levels of arsenic found in your system were not high at all, obviously because that would've been fatal. It was just enough to make you sick however." She smiled like it was no big deal. Maybe it wasn't a big deal health wise, but the fact that I threw up so violently was a big fucking deal to me.

"Okay, thank you," I nodded and she left.

Max came in after about thirty minutes and hugged me tightly.

"Max, I can't do this anymore, she tried to kill me!" I cried.

"Shhhh, calm down Namiko, you're overreacting," Max said.

"What? It was arsenic Max!" I shouted.

"I know Nami, but the doctor told me it was probably the water you were consuming or the rice that was used," he shrugged.

"Why didn't anyone else get sick? Aren't we all drinking the same thing? Didn't everyone else eat the soup?" I frowned.

"No, no one ate the soup but you," he sighed. "I know how this looks, but give her the benefit of the doubt like she gave you after the cheesecake incident." He rubbed my shoulder. I didn't respond and just stared off.

I was released the next day, and luckily, MJ and I were fine. I was terrified of Max's mother, and I didn't want her to be around MJ or me any more. I didn't care what she or anyone else said, she and I were a done deal and there was nothing she or Max could do to change it.

KIYUKI

I had a feeling Deshawn was still messing with Evelyn, so I wanted to find out for sure. I followed him today, and sure enough we ended up at her house. Once I found a park, I shut my engine off, and made myself comfortable.

He handed her a box of stuff, as I watched intently. She took the box into the house after they exchanged words, and he followed her. Tears welled up in my eyes, but I wiped them away.

This is why I used niggas, because all they did was use you. To think I was sad about fucking Larry, when he was playing me this whole. I shook my head, and sped off to my next destination.

That guy Chris was still in hiding, and I knew Max would find him soon. I would kill him myself, but I wasn't the killing type. I didn't know anything about hiding the body and not getting caught, so that was out of the picture. I pulled up to his apartment complex, and checked my makeup. I walked out, and up his steps, and then knocked on the door. As soon as he opened it, he pulled me in.

"I'm surprised you're staying at home," I chuckled.

"This ain't my crib! Max and them have already been through that shit," he exhaled and sat down.

"Oh," I nodded and sat next to him.

"So what did you hit me for?" He looked over at me as he rolled a blunt.

"I wanted to talk to you because I know sooner or later, Max is gonna catch you," I replied.

"How do you know?" he frowned.

"I'm his sister-in-law, I know," I half lied.

"Okay, so what?" he shrugged.

"So in order to not go down for this alone, you should let them know who hired you. Meaning tell them it was only Larry," I said.

"Why would I do that?" he scoffed.

"Because he's scared shitless right now, and is about to tell them where you are," I lied.

"I knew I couldn't trust his bitch ass," he grimaced.

"Now, I'm doing you a favor by telling you-" Deshawn calling me interrupted my sentence. I ignored it then put it in my purse. "Like I was saying, I'm telling you because I want you to be up on game. That way if you do get caught up, you know who fucked you over," I said and he nodded as he lit his blunt.

"Well I appreciate that Kiyuki," he smirked.

"So do we have a deal that you don't know me?" I raised a brow.

"Almost..." he bit his lip.

"What do you mean almost?" I frowned.

"I need a little something extra," he smiled, and his dimples appeared.

"Extra? I'm saving your life in a way. I'm letting you know that Max and Deshawn are gonna find you!" I exclaimed.

"Hey, niggas die every day. I ain't worried about dying," he chuckled and took a pull.

"Now I'm tryna get some, is you down or nah?" He raised both of his brows.

"If I do this, you won't tell?" I quizzed.

"I won't even remember what you look like," he replied and zipped his mouth with his fingers.

"Come on," I exhaled and stood up.

I went back to the room, and took my jeans off. He walked over, and pulled my panties down before taking my clit into his mouth. I threw my head back, as he tried to bring me to an orgasm. For some reason I felt guilty, even though I knew Deshawn was playing me. After licking me for hours it seemed, he dropped his pants and I handed him a condom. I didn't trust these niggas' condoms. He snatched it from me, and rolled it down. He laid on top of me and started to pump away immediately.

"Arrggghhhhhhh," he grunted and trembled as he nutted. I didn't get mine, but I didn't care. He bear hugged me, as he jerked every now and then. "Damn this is some good shit," he said as he rolled off of me.

I hopped up and ran to the bathroom to wipe up my pussy, before I went home and showered. I went and put my jeans on, then slid into my sandals.

"Remember our deal," I said.

"Who are you again?" he smirked. I smiled and nodded before heading home.

When I got home, I ran a bubble bath and then pulled my phone out of my purse. Deshawn was blowing me up, but I refused to deal with him. I think he made me fall in love, something I'd tried to prevent all my life. I powered my phone off, and then poured myself a glass of the champagne I had sitting by the tub. I sunk down into the bubbles, and relaxed while Amina Buddafly sang over the bathroom. Life was about to look up for me, somewhat.

DESHAWN

Kiyuki had me hot. I knew she saw me calling and texting, but she refused to hit me back or answer. I was gonna go over her house last night, but I chose no to. I didn't want to seem like some psycho ass nigga. However, tonight was a different story. She gave me the cold shoulder all day, while Evelyn blew me up.

I left from Max's house, and then drove about one-hundred miles per hour to Kiyuki's place. I ran up her walkway, and then beat on the door.

"What?" she scowled as she opened the door.

She had on a short silk nightgown, and her hair was in a loose bun. Her light skin looked freshly moisturized. I walked in, and she closed and locked the door behind me.

"Why you ain't been answering my calls?" I asked as I sat on her couch. She sat on the same couch, but further away, and folded her arms.

"Because I'm done with you," she replied staring straight ahead. I scooted closer to her, and threw my arm around her.

"Why babe?" I inquired as I saw a tear run down her light cheek.

"Because you lied! You're still with Evelyn," she sobbed. I didn't even know this woman cried.

"Come here girl. I didn't lie," I said as I hugged her tightly.

"I saw you yesterday! I followed you to her house!" she sniffled.

"I was dropping her stuff off," I replied.

"You followed her in!" she shouted.

"Only for a second. I grabbed the little stuff I had at the crib and left. Didn't you see me come right out?" I frowned.

"I left," she whispered and wiped her tears. I wiped the others and kissed her lips.

I dipped my tongue into her mouth, and rubbed my hands up her smooth thighs. "I missed you," I said in between kisses. I moved her panties to the side, and stuck my finger in her. I immediately snatched it out and stared at her.

"What?" she frowned.

"You fucked somebody else?" I glared at her.

"Deshawn I-"

"Did you fuck another nigga? I told you what it was!" I yelled.

"It was only because I thought you cheated! I'm sorry!" she cried. "How did you know?" she asked.

"I just do, and I ain't about to tell you how." I exhaled and dropped my head in my hands.

"Baby I'm sorry. Let's start over. I promise I won't do anything like this again. I love you," she said as she rubbed my back. I picked my head up and saw tears rushing out of her slanted honey eyes.

"You what?" I smiled.

"You heard me," she chuckled lightly.

"Say it again," I said as I pulled her into my lap.

"I love you Deshawn," she sniffled.

"Damn," I said as I rubbed her back. "I love you too, baby."

I lifted her up, and carried her to the bedroom. We undressed and I kissed and licked every part of her body. I climbed between her trembling legs, and positioned myself at her opening.

"Wait Desha-" she tried to say as I pushed myself inside her. I knew her pussy was good, but raw was even better. This pussy was magnificent. I stroked her slowly as we sucked each other's lips. "Don't cum in me," she whispered. I chuckled at her and kept working her walls. "I'm cumming baby..." she cried out right before her body jerked.

"I swear you better not give this pussy away ever again," I grunted, as I listened to my dick plow into her wetness.

I took her nipple into my mouth, and sucked and bit the both of them hungrily. "Oooh," she purred. I felt her soak my dick again, and I knew I wasn't gonna make it much further.

"Where can I cum?" I whispered in her ear as I licked it.

"Anywhere baby," she cooed as her small hands rubbed my muscular back. I sped up just a little, and then busted all in her guts.

"Deshawwwnnnn!" she panted. "I said don't cum in me!" she whined as I kissed her neck and squeezed her thighs.

"You said anywhere," I replied.

"Yeah, anywhere outside of me," she said as I kissed down her flat stomach. I licked and bit her inner thigh, as I made my way back to her pussy. "I hate you," she whispered.

"You what?" I asked before taking her clit into my mouth.

"I ha-hate yoouuuu!" she cried out as I pushed her legs back to fuck her with my tongue. "Ohhh. I love you," she switched it up quickly.

MAXIMILIAN

This evening was a happy ass evening for me. I sat outside of the current apartment that this nigga Chris lived in. Once I killed him, the last of the niggas who shot at me would be gone. I was hoping that he would tell who hired him though. Nah fuck that, he was going to tell me. Especially since I had a torture chamber set up for that ass back at the warehouse if he refused.

Deshawn and I got out of the car, and ran up the steps to his door. I knocked lightly, and then Deshawn and I moved from the view of the peephole.

"Aye, who is it?" the nigga yelled and neither of us answered.

He must've walked away after that, because we didn't hear anything else. I knocked again, and then hid like before. Finally, the door swung open.

"Aye who the fuck-" he paused when he saw my gun his face.

Deshawn and I barged into his crib, and then Deshawn locked the door.

"You thought I wasn't gone find you?" I smirked.

"Nah, I knew you was coming sooner or later," he chuckled.

"Good," I said as I shot his shoulder.

"Fuck! Just kill me man!" he shouted as blood gushed out over his fingers.

"Nah, I need to know who sent you," I glared at him.

"Ya homeboy!" he snickered and fell back onto his couch in pain.

"Who?" Deshawn frowned.

"Larry. Ya boy," he panted as held his shoulder.

"How do I know you ain't lying?" I asked hoping he was. Larry was my nigga, and he seemed to be cool even after I fired his incompetent ass.

"Check my phone. Fuck!" he shouted and looked over his bleeding shoulder.

I nodded towards the phone, and Deshawn picked it up to scroll through it. He paused and appeared to be reading, as I kept my gun pointed at Chris.

"Man, this nigga Larry." Deshawn smacked his lips and exhaled heavily.

I shot the dude between the eyes, and then Deshawn and I dipped out to Larry's. I didn't need a clean-up crew, because unfortunately, we lived in the murder capital, and this shit happened everyday. The law enforcement didn't give a fuck about a dead black man. To them, we were all just a bunch of gang bangers anyway. The gloves we wore were protection enough though.

We pulled up to Larry's crib, and then headed up to his house. I banged on his door with my fist, and made sure my gun was hidden. Deshawn did the same.

"Hey, what's up y'all?" Larry grinned nervously.

"What's up homie?" I smiled back.

"Why are y'all wearing gloves?" He frowned before realizing what we were here to do. "Aye nigga, I ain't do shit. This was all Kiyuki's idea!" he said with his hands up.

"Nigga, shut yo' mouth up about my girl," Deshawn shouted.

"Old boy ain't say nothing about Kiyuki, and neither did y'all text conversation," I said waving my gun. "And how did you know why we were here to kill you if you ain't do shit?" I raised a brow and he was speechless.

Deshawn turned on his silencer, and pumped two in his head.

Because Larry lived close to Chris' hideout, we did call clean up. Two murders so close together may get the attention of the police. They may think it was a serial killer on the loose and we ain't need that.

Once the crew did their job, Deshawn and I headed to the warehouse to check on our hostages. When we walked in, it was quiet as hell, which could be a good thing or a bad thing. I let out a sigh of relief as I walked into the corner room to see Cobra's mother and sister still tied up. I peeled the tape off of their mouths, and then sat down to stare at them. I picked up the new dummy phone I'd just copped, and snapped a picture of them. I sent it to Cobra and waited for his response.

"Why are you doing this mijo?" his mother cried.

"Your son fucked with someone he shouldn't have," I replied and exhaled. I was tired as hell.

"Please, let my mother go. I will do anything," Esmeralda sobbed. I don't know what she thought this was, but her good looks weren't gonna get her out of this. "My mother is sick; she needs her medicine," she added. I went ahead text what she'd said to Cobra.

"I just told your brother that, so if he cares he will show his face," I shrugged.

"What's wrong with her?" Deshawn inquired.

"Sh-she-"

"She's lying," I chuckled.

"No, she has diabetes and her blood sugar needs to be monitored." Esmeralda shot daggers at me.

My phone buzzed and I flipped it open.

Cobra: *Just give me the product.*

This nigga was scared as hell. He was too pussy to even save his own family.

"We'll see you ladies tomorrow," I said as Deshawn and I got up.

"Pleeaaassse!" they begged and cried.

We ignored them and went out to the car. I stopped at the party store, bought some chips and water, and then took it back to their asses. They both thanked me as I gave them the chips and water. After they ate and drank, we tied their asses back up.

"Someone will be here tomorrow for breakfast," I spat.

"Can it be you?" Esmeralda smirked. I walked back over to her, and taped her mouth up before leaving.

"I just need to stop by Red Sugar and make sure it's good," I told Deshawn while we were in the car, and he nodded.

I walked into the place, and thank God it was finally popping again.

"Aye Max," Gordon jogged over to me. "Ya step daddy in here refusing to pay the young lady for the dance he just got," he said.

"My step daddy? Nigga what?" I looked him up and down like he was crazy. Gordon pointed over to a table, and I saw Alfred's bitch ass sitting down nursing a drink.

"Get the fuck out," I said as I snatched his drink.

"Son," he smiled.

"I ain't your fucking son!" I shouted. "Get the fuck up and get out!" I said as I grabbed him up by his collar.

I damn near dragged him towards the door, and threw him outside. He laughed and stumbled over a little, then wandered off somewhere. What the fuck!

"Who didn't he pay?" I asked Gordon.

"Candy," he replied.

I walked over to her and she hugged me.

"How much does he owe you?" I asked her.

"Just $90," she replied and shook her head.

I peeled off a solid hundred, and handed it to her. "Keep the change," I said. "Sorry about that baby girl," I added and she kissed my cheek.

"Thank you Max," she beamed and switched off.

I rushed outside and was happy to see Alfred was nowhere in sight.

"Let's go," I told Deshawn.

❧

IT WAS 12AM WHEN I GOT HOME, BUT MY BABY GIRL WAS STILL awake.

"Finally," she smiled as the TV lit up her face. I chuckled and then went to shower.

When I came out, Namiko was sleep with the covers off of her. I missed making love to her with our bodies touching. Her belly had been in the way, and now that it was gone, my dick bricked up at the thought. I climbed in bed, and turned her on her back.

"What Max?" she whispered as I took her gown off.

I pulled down her panties, and kissed her stomach. I laid down on her, and wrapped her in my arms tightly as I entered her.

"Spread your legs some more," I ordered so that I could get all the way in.

"Uhh," she moaned.

"I missed this Nami," I whispered into her mouth as we kissed.

The feeling of her hard nipples against my body, almost made me nut on contact. Her skin was so soft, and being against it again felt euphoric. I pulled her hair out of its bun, and stared down into her beautiful face as I thrust into her. She caressed my face as we kissed like maniacs, and wrapped her legs around my waist.

NAMIKO

Right when I was all healed up, Maximilian came and fucked the shit out of me. Now I'm sore between the legs again, but it's not as bad as childbirth I must say.

"Good morning," I smiled as I walked into Baby Max's room.

I picked him up, and kissed his fat cheeks. He was the cutest baby in the world. Gwendolyn was right about him not looking Japanese; however, he did have my honey eyes.

"I love you," I beamed as I cuddled him.

I sat down in my rocking chair, and then began to breast feed him as I rocked back and forth.

"Hey babe," Max walked in.

"Hi," I whispered as he kissed my lips.

"Look at you," he smirked. "So how is school going?" he asked.

"It's fine. Especially since I only have one class per day," I said as I checked my baby.

"Well, baby, today I can't watch him while you're in class," he replied.

"Oh, I see. Well I just won't go today," I half smiled.

"Or my mom could watch him," he offered.

"No Max," I responded sternly.

"Baby, she didn't poison you," Max pleaded.

"Oh, then who did?" I shouted in a whisper.

"The doctor explained what happened Nami. You're being ridiculous," he smiled.

"And you believe that she didn't poison me on purpose?" I scoffed. "Your mother has turned psycho," I added. I hated that he thought our feud was comical.

"So you're just gonna cut her out of his life forever?" he quizzed ignoring my question.

"No. He can see her when he's in his twenties," I nodded.

"Namiko!"

"Shhhh!" I frowned. "He's not going over there. It's no telling what she would do to him," I said.

"Aight, I'm out." Max turned to leave.

"When will you be back?" I asked.

"Maybe tomorrow," he said and walked out.

I unlatched MJ from my nipple, and then put him in the crib. I fixed myself, and then rushed out to Max.

"Really?" I frowned once I walked into the kitchen to see him pouring some pop.

"What are you talking about?" He turned his lip up as if he was disgusted.

"You're mad at me now?"

"Yeah, because you're being ridiculous," he replied and poured some more into his cup before putting it away.

"Baby, I'm not. I'm scared for him to be over there after what happened," I said as I neared him.

"Whatever," he scoffed and left the kitchen before I could touch him.

I went back upstairs and gave MJ a bath, before bringing him into the den with me.

"Hey Nami, I'm leaving," Aniku peeked her head in.

"Oh, okay. Where?" I smiled.

"I'm going to the park with Konz," she blushed.

"Is that your boyfriend?" I quizzed.

"No, he's like my best friend," she chuckled.

"Do you guys have sex?" I inquired.

"No Nami! Not until marriage, remember?" She grinned and sat next to MJ to kiss his cheek.

"So you wouldn't be mad if I said I saw him with another girl yesterday," I tested her.

"You did?" She swallowed a lump.

"No, but by your reaction I can tell that you like him." I raised a brow.

"Maybe a little bit, but I know he's a player." She dropped her head.

"Yeah, he is," I exhaled.

"Has he said that he likes you, too?" I questioned.

"Yeah, he says that he does but who knows with Konz," she laughed.

"He is a wildcard." I shook my head. "Well, I don't want to keep you." I smiled and rubbed her thigh.

"Okay. Bye." She hopped up and kissed my cheek before leaving.

I relaxed all day with my baby. I tried to get Evelyn to come over but she was too depressed about Deshawn. I picked up my phone, and then dialed Kiyuki. She'd been calling and texting for over a month and I never responded.

"Hey baby sister," she sang into the phone.

"You sound happy," I smiled.

"I am," she replied.

"Oh, well, I was wondering if you wanted to come over and see my son," I offered.

"Yeah, when?" she beamed.

"Right now?" I asked more so than stated.

"Okay, on my way," she said and we hung up.

I made us some barbecue beans and meat because that used to be our favorite meal when we were six and eight.

"Something smells good," Kiyuki said as she walked into the kitchen holding MJ.

"Beans and meat," I chuckled.

"Here we are years later still eating that." She nodded and laid MJ in his swing.

"I know," I replied as I made us a bowl of it.

"I'm sorry about the things I've said to you Nami. You were right, I was miserable," she exhaled, as we ate at the island in the kitchen. "You know I would never sleep with your husband behind your back. I'm happy for you guys."

"Thank you. And it's okay, I'm just glad we're back to normal." I touched her hand, and she kissed the back of mine.

We talked all night, until she left to go be with Deshawn. I felt bad being in the middle of she and Evelyn's drama. I just hoped Deshawn wasn't gonna go back and forth between the two, because that could get ugly. However, it didn't look like he was coming back to Ev anytime soon.

It was 5am when I heard Max walk into the bedroom. He changed into his pajamas and left out. Our room was dark, so he thought I was asleep and didn't see him. I got up, and looked out the bedroom door to see him go into the guest room. I followed him, and then climbed into the bed with him.

"Are you still mad?" I asked as I straddled him.

"Yeah," he responded in a low tone.

I kissed down his dark caramel chest, as his hands squeezed my ass. I went back up to his lips, and kissed him slowly and gently.

"Don't be mad," I whispered as I rocked my hips, dry humping him.

He ripped my panties, and slid into me. Between him and Alfred, I was gonna have to go panty shopping soon. I sat up and removed my t-shirt as I rode him slowly. He ran his hand up my stomach, and cupped my small breasts.

"Damn you're sexy," he commented, as he stared at me lustfully. I still had a little stomach when I was in the sitting position, so I was happy that it didn't turn him off. "You're so sexy in any shape," he said as if he read my mind. I was used to having a flat toned stomach though, and I couldn't wait to get it back. He flipped me on my back and sucked my neck. "I love you. Everything about you Namiko," he whispered and sent chills down my spine.

He worked in and out of me in a circular motion, making me cum hard as hell. He put me on all fours, and spread my ass cheeks as he plowed into me.

"Ahhhh! Ahhh!" I called out as he reached around and played with my clit.

He licked my asshole, and then up my spine while not breaking his stride. He gripped my waist tightly, and fucked me hard and fast while smacking and grabbing my ass cheeks.

"Fuck Nami," he groaned. I spread my legs some more as I felt my orgasm rising.

"Oohhhh!" we cried out together, as he let loose inside of me, and I gushed on his rod.

He kissed my neck from behind, and then put me on my back. I lightly pushed him off, and then took his dick into my mouth.

ANIKU ALLEN

I'd been hanging out with Konz constantly. I didn't really know him like that, but when I moved in with Namiko and Max, we started getting closer. He always came over to see his brother, and the couple times that Max wasn't there, he started to chill with me while he waited for him. One thing led to another, and now we we're like Siamese Twins damn near. Sometimes I would tell Namiko that I was hanging out with my friend Orianna, but I was really going to see him. I liked him a lot, but I knew he was the one-nighter type, and I was not gonna give up my virginity to a nigga like that. If only he could be more like his older brother.

"You look sexy today," Konz smiled at me as I walked into his house.

I hated when he talked to me like that, because it made me want to do things that I shouldn't be doing. As soon as we sat on the couch, he darted his tongue into my mouth and rubbed his hand up my shirt.

"Konz!" I whined as I tried to push his ass off me.

Konz was fine as fuck. He was brown skinned, with full lips, and perfect white teeth. He was muscular, dressed nice, and always had a fresh fade. I liked how wild he was, and he liked how wild I wasn't.

"When are we gon' have sex Aniku?" he whispered as he kissed my face.

"I can't," I panted, feeling my panties become soaked.

"Why, cause of Namiko?" he smacked his lips.

"No, because my parents taught me to wait until I'm married," I nudged him.

"Married? A nigga like me don't get married," he smiled and bit his bottom lip.

"And that's why I will never have sex with you." I rolled my eyes.

"Well, you should at least let me take your virginity. After that, I won't bother you," he replied and held his hands up in mock surrender.

"Why the hell would I do that? Did you hear anything I said?" I frowned.

"Yes, but any nigga that waits until marriage is a square and probably has no strokes. I'm offering you this one-time special deal to get that pussy stroked the right way, before you get locked down by some weak ass nigga," he smirked. I stared at him for a little bit, and then burst into laughter.

"You're really serious?" I cheesed and he nodded.

"I am," he said and rubbed his hand up my leg.

"No Konz," I giggled and pushed his hand.

"You gone give me some pussy one day. Maybe when your nerdy husband is at work," he said, scratching his head and flipping through the TV channels.

"Your brother waited for Nami, is he a square?" I raised a brow.

"They got married quick as fuck. And when they did, that nigga couldn't even make it back to Detroit before he was knocking that shit out the frame," he laughed.

"Ugh! How do you know?" I turned my lip up.

"Cause she was walking like these bowlegged hood rats out here," he chuckled lightly.

I shook my head as I remembered how she *was* walking a little funny that day Max dumped her off at home to "handle business".

"Well regardless, I'm not having sex with you." I got up and went to his fridge to get some pop. As soon as I sat down and sipped it, he snatched it from me and drank some out. "Stop!" I whined and snatched it back. "You drank half the can!" I frowned.

"You'll be aight." He burped as his phone chimed.

We both looked down and I saw some chick named Ayanna had texted him. He chuckled when he saw me roll my eyes.

"Who is that?" I asked as he typed away.

"A little something something," he shrugged.

"Y'all have sex?" I inquired.

"Hell yeah. You're the only girl I spend time with and don't get the coochie." He looked over at me with his sexy ass.

"Don't say coochie, that sounds dirty." I twisted my lips and then sipped my pop.

"I bet yours is sweet though." He bit his lip and rubbed my thigh.

"Konz," I whispered as he pecked my lips.

He took my grape pop out of my hand, and set it on the coffee table, as he dipped his tongue into my mouth. He reached down into my tube top, and released my small breasts. His warm mouth felt so good, as he wrapped his lips around my hard nipples. He cupped them in his hands and switched back and forth, sucking each one hungrily. He stopped, and looked up at me before devouring my lips. I pulled my tube top up, and then pushed him back.

"Damn I wanna fuck you," he sighed and sat back. "I wanna fuck the shit out of you," he added and shook his head. I just laughed and shook my head as well. "I swear if you ever let me fuck, I'm gone have you in that room for a full week," he scoffed and smiled.

I just exhaled heavily, hoping I could hold out longer. I couldn't believe I'd just let him do what he'd just done. *Slow your roll Aniku,* I told myself.

KIYUKI

Since Deshawn and I were officially together exclusively, he wanted to take me out on an official date. It was our way of starting the relationship fresh. I'd only allowed him to take me to the movies or the mall, but no fancy restaurants. I was a little nervous because like I said, I'd never been on a date before with someone I loved. I've had expensive dinners, shopping trips, and gifts, but nothing like what I was probably gonna experience tonight. I think I was nervous because I cared about Deshawn, and most importantly, I was in love with his light bright ass. I smiled to myself as I tied my halter dress straps behind my neck.

I unclipped my hair, and then placed it into a nice messy bun, a little above the nape of my neck. I wore my most comfortable heels because I didn't want to ankle-break or do anything else embarrassing. I don't know why I was acting like this was the first time I'd ever hung out with this nigga.

I was putting my lipstick on, when the doorbell rang. I mushed my lips together to even out the color, and then took a deep breath before answering the door.

"You look good as usual." Deshawn smiled and kissed my lips lightly.

"Thanks," I grinned and grabbed my small purse.

He handed me some flowers, and I was already getting hot inside. He looked so good in a button up sweater, light blue jeans, and Nikes. He was pretty but still had that thug edge that all the girls liked.

"You look nice too babe," I smirked.

"Of course," he jerked his head back.

"I'm never complimenting your ass again," I chuckled, as we walked to the car.

He opened the door for me like always, and then jogged around so we could leave. He'd already told me prior, to let him do all the planning and not to ask any questions. I told him I had never been on a date with anyone I cared about, so he was excited to pop that romantic date cherry.

We pulled up to a big blueish-gray house after about thirty minutes. It was so beautiful, and I could tell the paint job was fresh.

"De-"

"Ah!" He cut me off and smiled as he got out of the car.

He opened my door and helped me out. We walked up the long driveway, and he stuck a key in the door. I prayed to God that this wasn't a set up. When we walked in, the house was somewhat empty and somewhat furnished. We continued to the dining area, which was fully furnished and fixed up. There was a chef standing in the room, smiling from ear to ear.

"Good evening, Mr. Sinead," he nodded and Deshawn nodded his head up to him.

Deshawn pulled my chair out, and then went to sit down across from me. The chef poured us some glasses of champagne, and then gave us some time to chat.

"Deshawn whose house is this?" I whispered.

"I just bought it," he smirked and sipped his champagne.

"But why? You already had a house," I frowned.

"I uh, had to leave that place," he sighed.

"Leave it for Evelyn?" I raised a brow.

"Why do you want to talk about that? Let's talk about something else," he smiled.

"Deshawn, you better not be still fucking her," I replied getting hot all over.

"Baby, I'm not." He grabbed my hands and rubbed them. "I love you, girl," he whispered as he stared into my eyes.

"You love me?" I blushed.

"Yeah, I do. I kind of hated you when we first met, so it's crazy how far we've come," he said.

"Why did you hate me?" I asked.

"I felt like you were a shady rat." He turned his lip up in disgust.

"Well I'm not," I spat clearing my throat.

"I think you had a little rat in you, but not anymore," he responded as I sipped my champagne.

"If you think I had some rat in me, why are you my man?" I inquired.

"Because we naturally became close when I woke up from that coma. I wanted to give us a try, despite my reservations," he said.

I cringed lightly at the sound of his coma. I couldn't believe I was once responsible for trying to kill him.

"You probably still think I'm a hoe," I joked.

"Nah, I don't. If I did, I wouldn't be hitting it raw." He bit his lip.

"Yeah, we may have to stop that," I smiled.

"No, that pussy is way too good. You got me hooked already. Don't do that," he laughed, and so did I.

The chef brought our dishes twenty minutes later, and we stuffed our faces. For dessert, we had raspberry cheesecake, and it was to die for. As we walked out of the dining room, Deshawn scooped me up, and carried me upstairs to the bedroom.

"Deshawn, you don't even have a bed in here," I chuckled.

"Not yet." He put me down and then went to get his blow-up mattress.

"When will this be furnished?" I quizzed.

"In two days, but I still wanted to have our date," he panted as we watched the bed inflate.

"Too embarrassed to take me out?" I smiled.

"Never. I just wanted to be in an intimate setting with you," he replied.

"Yeah right." I smacked my lips and leaned up against the wall.

"I will take you to the busiest place in Detroit for breakfast tomorrow," he chuckled.

"You better," I responded as he neared me.

He pinned me against the wall, and pecked my lips lightly. He slid his tongue into my mouth, as he raised my dress over my head. He tugged my panties down, making sure not to break our kiss. He stepped back and removed his clothes as I watched. His chiseled abs looked painted on because they were so perfect. He walked back up to me, dick swinging, and carried me to the bed.

"Look at that food baby," he chuckled. My stomach was usually flat as hell, but we had really pigged out.

"Shut up," I pouted playfully as he kissed my small bulge.

"I'm gone put a real one in there," he said before placing my legs on his shoulders.

He sucked on my clit gently, while holding my legs apart with his strong hands.

"Deshawnnnn," I whispered as he licked and sucked me like the champion pussy eater he was. I had never had head this good. "Fuck babe," I whined, feeling my pelvis tighten. "Uuggghhhhh," I grunted softly as I exploded. He licked up all my juices, and then began to suck my clit again while dipping his finger into my hole.

"My pussy tastes so good," he said between working his tongue.

"Ahhhh! Uhhh!" I cried out as I came yet again. He gave me one last lick, and then stood up on his knees.

I sat up, and took his eleven inches into my mouth. I slobbered on it, letting my spit coat the whole thing. "Shit," he groaned as he watched me work my jaws. He slowly humped my face as I bobbed my head and massaged his balls at the same time. "You gone swallow for daddy?" he asked biting his lip. I looked up at him and nodded slowly. "Fuck." He threw his head back as I really started to show out. "Yuki fuck!" he damn near screamed, as he spilled his nut down my throat. I swallowed it up like it was gonna be my last drink on Earth. "Tonight I'm gonna fuck you," he said as he kissed me roughly.

He flipped me over, spread my legs, and then slid into me from behind. He grabbed my ass, spread my cheeks, and plowed into me hard and fast.

"Put the side of your face in the pillow," he ordered.

I did as he asked, and we made eye contact as he fucked my brains out. This nigga was gonna have me fighting bitches over this dick like Evelyn. He spanked me hard, making me bite my lip.

"You're so fucking sexy," he growled when he saw me do so.

"Ohhhh! I love you Deshawn!" I moaned loudly.

"Whose pussy is this?" he asked while biting his lip.

"Yours, daddy," I shouted as I came on his thick rod. Our skin smacking was so loudly I was sure the chef heard it downstairs.

"Stay still," Deshawn panted as he drilled into me.

He pulled me upward, so that my back was against his chest. He cupped my breasts, while moving his hips in a circular motion. He sucked my bottom lip before throwing me back down to finish breaking my back.

"Oh my gosh, this is some good ass pussy," he yelled and wrapped my hair around his hand.

"Ahhhhhhh!" we screamed together as we both released.

"Babe, I released so much into you. I'm sure you're pregnant," he chuckled out of breath. He slid out of me slowly, as I tried to catch my breath. "My handprint is on your ass," he laughed, as he plopped down next to me. *I swear, the struggles of being a light bright,* I thought.

"That was the best, Deshawn," I finally spoke.

"I know. That's why I'm your man and that pussy has my name on it," he said standing up.

"Where are you going?" I asked. I was hoping he wasn't about to take me home, and possibly run home to Evelyn.

"We're about to take a shower. Calm down," he said as he helped me up.

"I was making sure you weren't trying to run back to your ex and double dip," I half joked.

"Kiyuki, you're my one and only, aight?" he said, as he pulled me close. I nodded my head. "Nah, say it."

"Aight," I smiled and he kissed me passionately.

When we got out the shower, I heard my phone go off in my purse.

I didn't want it to disturb us for the rest of the night, so I retrieved it to power it down. I saw it was Cori again, so I opened it up.

Cori: *Enjoy it while it lasts hoe. My brother is gonna hate you soon.*

I quickly turned my phone off, and went to lay down with Deshawn. I was starting to get worried because she seemed to know more about me than I initially thought.

MAXIMILIAN

Although I had a gym at home, I was going to 24-hour Fitness tonight because Namiko said my weights and stuff were waking the baby up. Our house was way too big, but since she had hearing like a dog, she felt everyone else did too. I'm pretty sure my son could sleep peacefully without me disturbing him with the clanking of weights, but whatever.

Anywho, it was 1am and I hated having to go out into the cold air, but I needed to keep my body strong after that accident. I usually would have some people watching my back, but I was only gonna be here for a couple hours, *and* it was late as fuck.

I pulled into the parking lot, which only had about four cars, and threw my shit into park. After grabbing my gym bag, I jogged inside to get my shit started.

"Hey," I heard someone say as I jogged on the treadmill shirtless. I looked to my left to see that nurse chick, Melissa.

Fuck, I forgot she worked out here. Why was she always here when I was? It's not like I came at the same time everyday.

"What's up?" I replied keeping my eyes on the TV straight ahead.

"You haven't been here in a while," she said as she started to walk slowly on the treadmill next to me.

"Yeah, because I have a gym at home," I panted trying to keep up my same running pace.

"Then why are you here?" she questioned.

"Because my wife thinks my workouts wake up the baby," I responded and grabbed my overhead headphones.

"Damn you're rude," she chuckled.

"How so?" I quizzed.

"I'm talking to you and you're just gonna listen to music." She flashed her pretty smile.

"My bad." I pursed my lips and set my earphones down. It was quiet for a couple minutes as I continued to run on the treadmill.

"Damn, an hour?" She raised a brow as she leaned over to look at the time on the machine.

"Yep," I replied, happy that it was time to get off and away from her.

"Where are you going?" she asked as I sipped my Gatorade.

"Upstairs for some leg, abs, and arm weights," I responded and rushed off.

After doing three hundred reps for my legs, I went over to do the same for my abs.

"Damn," I heard Melissa say as she appeared.

I usually didn't work out with my shirt off, but since the place was empty tonight, I'd left it in the car.

"I don't want to be rude, but I'm trying to work out in peace," I huffed.

"Aight daddy." She threw her hands up and switched off.

I was pretty sure she didn't have panties on under them skin tight ass work-out pants. Her fat ass was bouncing around with each step, and I had to snap myself out of the trance it was putting me in. I liked to look, but cheating on my wife was never gonna happen, no matter what. After three hundred crunches, and lifting weight reps, I decided to head home since I was getting sleepy.

As I was walking out, I felt someone walking behind me. I pretended not to see or hear Melissa's footsteps as I made it out into the cool air.

"Wait Max!" she finally called out.

"What?" I frowned and turned to look at her.

"Ah!" she screamed just as something heavy clocked me across the back of my head.

"Arrgghhhh!" The pain was excruciating and I was pretty sure that if it hit me again I'd be brain dead.

I turned around to see a Hispanic guy, and he raised the barbell again. Just as he was about to hit me, Melissa jabbed him in the eye with her little pink weight. He stumbled back, and she hit him again and again, until he passed out.

"I'm calling 911, babe!" she yelled as she dialed on her phone.

A 24-hour Fitness employee rushed out to check the scene. "Oh my goodness, are you okay?" she asked as she touched my head.

I glared at the nigga laid out on the floor, but I couldn't get up due to the blow to my head. I wanted to kill his ass, but I was somewhat out of commission and there were witnesses. On top of that, the ambulance was taking forever; typical for Detroit. They didn't give a fuck about black people or people in black neighborhoods.

"Let me drive you," Melissa offered as she and the employee helped me to my car.

I didn't want her driving my whip, but now was not the time to be petty. Melissa dipped through the streets swiftly, and we finally arrived to the hospital. As soon as they put me on the gurney, I passed the fuck out.

When I woke up, I was in a dark room and all I could hear were machines. I laid there for a couple more seconds, trying to gather my thoughts. I slowly sat up and looked around, although it was pitch black.

"Hello?" I called out groggily. Nothing. I cleared my throat before speaking again. "Hello!" I shouted.

Suddenly, a big metal door came open, and Deshawn walked in. He cut on the light, and it was like a decked out hospital room. I'd finally remembered that I had this shit built after that whole accident, because it was too dangerous for me and him to be in a hospital if something happened to us. I'd hired nurses and medical professionals to tend to Deshawn, our team, and me.

"You good?" he asked.

"Yeah, I'm good. We need to get Cobra," I exhaled.

"That's who did it?" he questioned.

"Yes. He sent some nigga to damn near kill me. Thank God Melissa's thirsty ass followed me," I shook my head. I felt bad for calling her thirsty since she technically saved my life.

"About that, your wife is on her way here." Deshawn chuckled and left before I could say anything.

Right after he left, the doctor I hired came to check on me, and the nurse brought me some lunch. I ate, and then got up to take a shower and brush my teeth. As I was climbing back into the hospital bed, Namiko came in.

"Hey baby," I smiled. She looked uncomfortable as she closed the door.

"Where is MJ?" I inquired.

"He's with Aniku," she replied somberly.

"What's wrong baby?" I frowned. "Come here," I added.

Her long dark hair was in a bun on her head, and she wore skinny jeans, sandals, and a t-shirt. Even in the simplest outfits she was breathtaking. She walked over to me slowly, and I pulled her into the bed with me. I kissed her soft lips, and let our tongues dance for a bit before she pulled away.

"Max, you said you went to the gym last night," she said looking up into my eyes. Her dark caramel complexion was nothing short of perfection.

"I did," I replied confused.

"Yeah, but you were with that nurse bitch," she said. I exhaled heavily because I knew this looked bad.

"Nami, I went to the gym and she was there. She was outside when I got attacked, and drove me to the hospital. I'm not sure how Deshawn got me here because I passed out, but I wasn't with her. You know I wouldn't fuck around on you," I pecked her soft lips.

"I know; I just want to know what happened," she sat up.

"Well I'm glad you know." I bucked my eyes, and then kissed her hand.

"I love you," she whispered as she pressed her forehead against mine.

"I love you more Mrs. Davis." I grabbed her and tongued her down good.

NAMIKO

Today, Gwendolyn and I were gonna go shopping together so we could have a big family dinner. It was kind of a way for us to start working on our horrible relationship. I was sure she hated me and was only doing this to please Max, but at this point I didn't really care what her reasoning was. I hated her ass too, and was only doing this for Max as well.

I dressed baby Max, and then placed him in his carrier. "Are you ready yet?" Gwendolyn rolled her eyes.

"Yes Ms. Gwen," I sighed, and grabbed the carrier.

We pulled up to Parkway Foods and got out. "Oh I have a basket," I told her as I placed MJ into the front part with his carrier.

"Yes, but we have different tastes I'm sure. You buy what you people eat, and I will buy what my people eat," she fake smiled.

"We're both black though," I replied confused.

"You're half, honey." She switched by me into the store.

One minute I was just a black chick, and the next I wasn't black enough. I threw my head back out of frustration, and then proceeded after her. I wanted to split up, but I knew the point in this whole disaster waiting to happen was for us to spend time and bond.

As we pushed our basket down the spices aisle, I spotted that nurse that helped Max. "Oh my goodness!" Gwendolyn shouted, causing the girl to look. "You saved my baby!" she beamed and hugged Melissa tightly.

"Oh, it was nothing," she grinned and then looked at me.

"Namiko! Have some manners. You should at least speak to the woman who saved your husband, unless you didn't want him to be saved." She raised a brow and folded her arms.

"Why wouldn't I want him to be saved?" I turned my lip up. She really said some stupid shit.

"I'm not sure, maybe you want money," she responded dumbly.

"Anyway, I appreciate you stepping in and saving my husband." I smiled and Melissa gave me a strange look.

"It was my pleasure. I didn't want anything happening to him. You know it was really late, and he shouldn't have been out." She shook her head.

"Yeah, I know. He just loves to keep his body together." I chuckled nervously because she and Gwendolyn were eye balling me.

"Yes, he told me you made him go out that night." She squinted her eyes at me in a suspicious manner. Gwendolyn gasped and scowled at me.

"Well, i-it was only because his equipment banging together wakes up the baby," I stammered slightly.

"You sent my baby out that night!" Gwendolyn hollered dramatically.

"Next time you may want to think about more than yourself when you make decisions like that," Melissa spat.

"You know, I would tell you to stop panting with your tongue out like a thirsty pit bull every time my husband comes around, but it looks like your desperation came in handy finally," I raised a brow. She raised hers as well, and scoffed as if she was appalled.

"Have a good day Ms. Gwen, and tell Max I said hello. I'll call to check on him soon," she said to my mother-in-law, but kept her eyes on me. She switched off as Gwendolyn shook her head.

"See, that's a real woman Namiko. Take notes," she said.

"I'm a real woman as well," I replied dryly as I looked at the spices.

"Oh, because you can lay on your back for my son?" She laughed as if it was hilarious.

"No! Because I carried his baby and pushed him out of my vagina!" I yelled louder than I wanted to. A couple people looked at me, and I just closed my eyes and took a breather. "Ms. Gwen, I am Max's wife. I'm going to be his wife for the rest our lives," I said.

"Until he realizes he can have someone like that young lady that saved him. You barely have breasts," she cackled.

"Max likes them just fine," I replied and bumped her with the basket.

Next thing I knew she was dumping a bottle of salt over my head. I jumped back quickly because I didn't want it to get on my son.

"What the fuck?" I scowled as she laughed. I took my water bottle, and doused her as she screamed.

"You little bitch!" she hollered and grabbed her water to do the same. I busted open a bag of flour ready to go to war. "You better not Namiko," she panted. I threw it straight in her face, and she fell back and slid down to the floor.

"Excuse me ladies what is-" the manager, I'm guessing, tried to say.

He was cut off when Gwendolyn charged me on the aisle. We were flying into the shelves, shouting and pulling on each other's hair. She slammed me into the canned soups, and my back ached. I finally decided to stop going easy on her old ass. I karate kicked her in the stomach, and she banged into the shelves filled with flour, and cake mixes. A couple bags busted open, and collapsed on her as she hit the floor.

"These two!" the guy yelled pointing to us.

Security grabbed us up, and Gwendolyn was literally all white.

"Wait! My baby!" I suddenly remembered as the two guards tried to whisk us away.

"Ma'am, I'm gonna let you get your baby, but you must leave," the security whispered in my face. I nodded and rushed to grab baby Max.

Once we calmed down, the men let us get in the car together. No words were spoken the whole ride home.

"WHAT THE FUCK HAPPENED?" MAX ASKED AS HE STARED AT ME. I knew I looked crazy, because my clothes were disheveled and wet.

"Your fucking mother! You better talk to her Max!" I shouted as I handed baby Max to him.

I ran upstairs and immediately cleaned myself up. When I walked out of the bathroom within our room, Max was on the bed, and MJ was in his swing in our room.

"Baby what happened?" he frowned up his fine ass face. His dark caramel skin was red under, so I knew he was angry.

"She embarrassed me!" I cried.

"Shhh, don't cry Nami. How did she embarrass you?" he asked as he hugged me.

"She was smiling all in that nurse bitch's face, making it obvious that she didn't like me. And then she started telling me I wasn't a woman, and that the nurse was," I sobbed.

"Namiko, don't let that get to you." He whispered.

"She said I had no boobs," I pouted and he laughed. "Max!" I whined. He opened my towel, and dropped it to the floor.

"You have just the right amount," he replied.

"Really?" I sniffled and smiled.

"Yep." He lifted me up and laid me on the bed. He took my nipple into his mouth and began to suck gently.

"Maaxxx, not in front of the baby," I moaned.

He hopped up, took MJ to his room, and then came back. He climbed back on top of me, and began to kiss my neck.

"Are you gonna talk to her?" I asked.

"Yes Nami," he said in a low tone as he took my nipples back into his mouth.

He switched back and forth between the two, as he fingered me slowly. He spread my legs wider, and fingered me faster until I came.

"See, only real women can cum that hard." He bit his lip as he undressed. "You're definitely a real woman baby. Having my baby, and then still looking the way you do," he said, as he kissed on my stomach.

"Yeah?" I whispered.

"Oh yeah," he said before taking my clit into his warm mouth.

DESHAWN

"Man, I think I found wifey," I chuckled, as Max and I chilled in his den.

"Damn, for real? I never saw the two of y'all linking up, but I guess you never know," he replied and I nodded.

"Yeah, she was the last person I was expecting to get involved with, especially since I had Evelyn," I sighed.

"Speaking of her, is that completely done?" he raised a brow.

"Yeah nigga. We've been broken up for months. She still hits me up for little shit, or she will pretend to accidentally text me. But get this, she and Kiyuki got into a fight at Target." I laughed and so did he.

"What the fuck? Nigga, I'm telling you right now, Evelyn ain't letting go that easy," he responded sternly.

"She don't have a choice," I shrugged.

"And you may not have a choice either," he joked. "Have you talked to your sister?" he asked.

"Nah, I don't know where or why her ass just up and disappeared," I said.

"Maybe because she was behind all that bullshit. You realize nothing has happened to Namiko since her ass has been M.I.A." He sipped his pop.

"I know, but I think it's just a coincidence. Shit, she's too busy beefing with ya moms anyway," I laughed.

"Ain't that the truth. I don't know what's wrong with my mother. She really dislikes Namiko for some reason. She swears she likes her, but I know she's just saying that for my benefit," he scoffed.

"Thank God my mama is down in Alabama," I replied sipping my beer.

"Maybe Cori is there, have you called?" He quizzed.

"Hell yeah nigga. Why are you so worried about my sister? You still on that?" I inquired.

"Nigga no, I'm happily married, aight?" he spat.

"I know I'm just making sure *you* remember that. You don't want Nami to hear you asking about Cori every hour on the hour," I half joked and we chuckled.

"Namiko knows what's up so she wouldn't care. She knows I'm all about her pretty ass," he smirked and I shook my head.

The front door slammed, and Max and I perked up.

"The hell," he said as he reached for his piece. He rose up, just as Konz came rushing into the den. "Nigga, you almost got lit up," Max exhaled as he plopped back down into his lazy boy. I relaxed as well.

"Big bro, I need a favor," Konz panted.

"A favor like what?" Max frowned.

"I need to borrow some cash," he said sitting down and running his hands over his face.

"I thought you had a hustle little nigga." Max shook his head.

"Look I do, now you gonna help me out or nah?" he spat.

"Aye muthafucka, remember you asking me for a fuckin' favor," Max barked.

"My bad, bro." Konz sat back.

"How much you need?" Max asked as he pulled his wallet from his basketball shorts pocket.

"The amount I need would not fit into that wallet," Konz replied.

"Nigga, what? How much do you need?" Max frowned in confusion.

"I need ninety grand." He clenched his teeth together, anticipating Max's response.

"You need ninety grand? For what?" Max shouted.

"Can I have it or not?" Konz scowled.

I wanted to find out what he needed it for too, but I decided against asking since it was a sibling thing.

"Nigga, you think you gone walk in here and ask me for almost one hundred thousand dollars and I ain't gone ask why? You out your rabid ass mind Konz," Max chuckled.

"Man, ninety grand ain't shit to you!" Konz yelled.

"It ain't about that. Regardless of how much money I have, ninety grand is a lot," Max responded. It was quiet for a little while as both brothers waited for the other to budge.

"Aight... if I tell you, will you promise not to get mad and just give me the cash?" Konz quizzed.

"Nope. But if you want to possibly get this money you better tell me anyway," Max scoffed. Konz took a deep breath, and then ran his hands over his face again.

"My umm, hustle was gambling. I-"

"Really Konz?" Max hollered.

"Nigga, let me finish!" Konz shouted. "Now like I was saying, I started doing it online and I was making a nice little amount of cash. Then I started doing it in person, and I'd been making a whole lot more money. This last time, I bet more cash than I had because I was for sure that I would win. To make a long story short, I lost, and now if I don't pay up these niggas are gonna kill me," he finished. I was biting my tongue so hard it was a surprise that I didn't have a mouth full of blood.

"You 'bout the dumbest nigga in Michigan," Max replied.

"I know man." Konz collapsed back into the couch.

"I'm gone give you this money, but this gambling shit ends here. If you get back into some shit, you're on your own. I usually would have those niggas killed, but why should they die because yo' stupid ass bit off more than you could chew. However, if they continue to threaten you, let me know and they'll be handled." Max stood up and left the den to retrieve the money.

"Shut up," Konz looked over at me.

"What? I ain't say shit!" I grinned.

"Yeah but I know you calling me all types of shit in your head," he responded.

"You right," I sipped my beer.

"I just need money man. This gambling shit was so easy, and I made a lot. If I quit, I don't know what I'm gonna do. I'm tired of living off of Max," he said.

"Get down with us," I said.

"I don't wanna do that shit!" He turned his lip up.

"Why?" I wondered.

"Because it's dangerous as hell. Bigger jail risk," he sighed.

"Konz, do you know who your brother is? He has more connects than the damn president. You come work with us you gone be good and paid," I nodded.

"He ain't got more connects than the president," he spat.

"Figure of speech dummy," I scoffed.

"He's sure living like the president," he said.

"Got you living like one too. It's time you get your own money, but with us," I replied.

Max walked in with a medium sized blue bag, and handed it to Konz. "Take this shit and go," he frowned and sat down.

"Thanks big bro. I promise this won't happen again. After I deliver this shit, I wanna see about getting down with you," Konz smiled.

"Dagger is waiting outside for you. He's gonna watch your back secretly while you deliver the money." Max waved his brother off, ignoring his last statement.

Konz just sighed and left the room.

KONSTANTIN "KONZ" DAVIS

❧

This gambling shit had been working for me for a while now. I didn't know if I could leave it alone, but I didn't want to risk being in the same situation again. Thankfully, the money was delivered to the niggas I owed safely, and everything was cool now. I was hoping Max didn't have to off their asses because then that would make me look even worse than I already did.

What Deshawn said was constantly on my mind though. I knew he and my brother made a lot of money, but that line of work seemed way more dangerous than the shit I was doing. Yeah, I know both could end up in jail time, but one was obviously worse.

I was chilling in my bed, texting a couple hoes that I had. I wanted some company, but I wasn't interested in having any of them come over. I was tired of smashing the same random hoes. I wanted something new, something like Aniku.

I hated that she knew what type of nigga I was, because she was keeping her legs closed tight. I've never wanted to fuck a bitch as bad as I wanted to fuck her. She was sexy as hell, with her smooth brown skin, long hair, slanted honey eyes, and perfect teeth. She was skinny, but I still liked her. My dick started to rise just from thinking about her.

I decided in my head that I would much rather have conversation than sex, so I shot Aniku a come over text instead of the hoes.

Aniku: *It's 11pm!*

Me: *You coming or nah?*

Aniku: *Fine.*

Me: *Hurry up, I want you to spend the night.*

Aniku: *You know I can't spend the night.*

Me: *Why?*

Aniku: *I don't want my sister getting suspicious.*

Me: *Say that you're with your homegirl.*

Aniku: *Okay.*

I smiled at my phone, and then went to hop in the shower.

Although Aniku was eighteen and I was twenty, it still seemed like I was waaay older than her. She was so sheltered, but I kind of liked that. She was a breath of fresh air compared to these Detroit hoes I usually fucked with.

I slipped on some boxers, basketball shorts, and socks, and then lit up a blunt. As soon as I finished it, I heard my doorbell ring. I ashed the blunt quickly, sprayed some breath spray, and then jogged to the door to answer it.

"Hey," Aniku smiled, as she adjusted her duffle bag strap on her shoulder.

"Hey." I bit my lip and watched her walk in and head to my bedroom. I pinched her little ass as she walked by and she yelped.

"So what was so important that I had to come over this late?" she raised her perfect brow.

"I just wanted to talk to you," I said closing my bedroom door.

Aniku took her jacket off, and she was wearing an oversized t-shirt, with jean shorts. I licked my lips at her smooth butter brown legs.

"Talk about what?" she asked.

"This gambling stuff. I can't do it anymore," I exhaled.

"Well, how are you gonna get money? You gonna work a 9-5?" she inquired. Aniku was the only person I told about my gambling. It seemed like we told each other everything.

"I don't know. I may just surrender and get down with my brother," I said turning on Netflix.

"I think it's safer for you," she caressed my face.

I looked over at her slowly, darted my tongue into her mouth, and then leaned her back on the bed. We sucked each other's lips, and let our tongues wrestle with each other. The kiss was hot and heavy, and my dick was taking notice. I unbuttoned her jean shorts, and pulled them to her knees.

"No, Konz," she finally said and pushed me off of her. I wanted, no I needed this pussy and I needed to find out how to get it before marriage.

"Come on babe, you know how I feel about you," I said as I kissed her neck.

I did have strong feelings for Aniku. I didn't know if it was love or what, but I definitely wanted her and all to myself. Yeah, I had no plans of being faithful but shit, a man is man. As long as I made sure she didn't know and that the hoes didn't get out of place, we would be good.

I kissed from her neck to her collarbone, and then reached up her shirt. I reached to unsnap her bra but she stopped me again.

"Is this why you called me over so late?" she frowned.

"What?" I frowned back.

"I'm not a booty call Konz. I'm not fucking you," she spat.

"Why?" I quizzed. I was so frustrated.

"Because I wanna wait until I'm married," she replied in a calm tone.

"But what if I loved you?" I inquired.

"You don't love me," she rolled her eyes.

"Yeah I do. That's why I spend all this time with you even though you don't give me none," I nodded. I was speaking to her, and realizing my feelings at the same time.

"You really love me?" she questioned.

"Yeah babe," I pecked her soft lips.

I tongued her down for a cool little minute, and then reached to unbutton her shorts again. She didn't stop me, and I was ecstatic. I pulled her shirt off and quickly unhooked her bra. I took her hard nipples into my mouth, and devoured them.

"Mmmmm," she moaned.

I continued to suck her nipples hungrily, while pulling her shorts to her ankles. I stood up, and lightly pushed her back. She stared at me with her beautiful ass, and I could tell she was scared. I pulled her little white panties down, which usually would've turned me off, but for some reason the fact that it was her wearing them, I didn't mind. I threw them across the floor, and just stood back to take in her small figure. I got on my knees, and spread her legs wide. I'd only eaten out one bitch and that was when I was fourteen years old. I ran my tongue across her pussy, and she tensed up.

"Relax so I can make you cum," I said.

I put her legs on my shoulders, and then took her clit into my mouth. I ran my tongue across her opening, and when I landed on the clit I sucked it gently.

"Konzzz," she whimpered.

I looked up at her as I French kissed her pussy, and her head was thrown back in ecstasy. She was propped up on her elbows, and breathing heavily. Her pussy tasted good as hell, and I guess it was because she had a good diet.

"Ahhh," she cried out as she came into my mouth. I kept licking between her hips, as her legs trembled on my shoulders. "Konz, I can't – uhhhh," she purred. She released again, and I licked her clean.

I wanted to have her suck my dick, but I didn't want her to change her mind about letting me fuck. I kissed her lower lips softly, and then stood up to take off my bottoms. I put her in the middle of the bed, and then climbed in between her legs after grabbing a condom. I stood on my knees to roll it down, and said a silent prayer thanking God for this moment.

"Is it gonna hurt?" she asked.

"Nah, you'll be good," I lied. I didn't want anything getting in the way of me popping this cherry tonight.

Once the condom was on, I lowered myself on top of her and slipped my tongue into her mouth. I pressed my head against her opening but it wouldn't let me in. I pushed one leg back, and then forced my way in by any means necessary.

"Konnnzzzzz," a tear slipped out of her pretty eyes, as I broke through her.

Anything in my way was getting ripped and busted through. She was so fucking tight, wet, and warm. I'd never felt pussy this tight in my life, but then again I'd never fucked a virgin. I was never interested. I pumped her slowly, until all ten inches of my dick was inside her little tight pussy. Tears continued to come out of her eyes as I thrust into her.

"Shit," I whispered as I slowly sucked her full lips.

"Uhhhh," she cooed into my mouth as I kissed her. "It hurts," she sniffled.

"Just give it time," I panted as I felt myself about to nut. *No, not yet Konz! You can't cum this quick on her first time,* I told myself.

"I'm gonna speed up a little baby," I told her once I composed myself.

"Not yet," she whispered. I hugged her body, darted my tongue into her mouth, and then beat her pussy up. Good Lord it felt good. "Mmmmmmm," she grunted into my mouth.

I kissed her hungrily to muffle her moans a bit, because she was damn near hollering. I felt her cum on my dick, and it made her pussy wetter. Fuck, I was out for the count.

"Argghhhhh!" I grunted loud as fuck like a lion or some shit.

My body jerked, and my toes curled and cramped up. FUCK! We kissed as we panted out of breath.

"That was so good Aniku," I closed my eyes and exhaled. Her chest heaved up and down as she tried to catch her breath as well.

"I love you," she looked into my eyes.

"I love you too," I replied and pecked her lips.

I slowly slid out of her, and the condom had blood on it. I went to flush it, then ran a bath in the Jacuzzi tub. I went to pick Aniku up bridal style, and then carried her to the tub. I put her in, and then climbed in with her. I pulled her between my legs, and then craned my neck around to kiss her lips. I wrapped my arms around her small torso and hugged her tightly against my chest. We stopped kissing, and she leaned against me.

"You know not to fuck nobody else right?" I asked to make sure and she nodded. "If I find out you fucked someone else, I'm gone kill both of y'all," I half joked and she chuckled. I reached around the front of her body, and cupped her small breasts in my hands as I kissed her cheek.

"So we're official now?" she inquired as she played with the bubbles.

"Yeah babe, you're my girl," I smiled to myself.

I couldn't wait to be fucking her 24/7. Shit, I may not have time for other females. But then again, I wasn't a one-woman type of nigga. I sighed at my thoughts, and then kissed the nape of Aniku's neck.

"That means no more hoes," she snapped me from my thoughts.

"Nope, just me and you, babe," I lied.

She turned to look at me, and had the prettiest smile on her gorgeous face. I hated to do her dirty, but I'm a man. Maybe one day I would settle down and make her my wife, but it wouldn't be anytime soon.

KIYUKI

I felt a little wetness between my legs, so I rushed to the bathroom. I quickly pulled my panties down, and sighed out of frustration. I was hoping I started my period but it wasn't anything there. Every little stomach pain I had, I was hoping it was cramps. I'd never wanted my period to come so bad. My in-love ass stopped making Deshawn use condoms, and I was neglecting my birth control.

"Shit!" I shouted.

I thought about taking a Plan B pill, but then I remembered those only worked within seventy-two hours of the sexual activity, and ain't no telling when he might have gotten me pregnant.

I pulled my panties up, and then lifted my shirt to see my flat stomach. I poked it out a little, and cocked my head to see what I would look like pregnant.

"You've been stressed Kiyuki, maybe it's just that," I said to myself.

Cori had been sending me weird ass texts, and I was on edge waiting for her to turn my life upside down. That had to be the reason my period wasn't here. I exhaled heavily, and then cut the light off and headed to my bedroom.

My phone buzzed and I saw it was a text from Deshawn saying he was on his way. I didn't feel like having company right now, but I knew he wouldn't take no for an answer. I got up and made a sub sandwich, then plopped down on the couch. I cracked open my grape pop, and took a big swig. Just as I was about to bite into the sandwich, the door-bell rang. I bit it anyway, and then hopped up to open the door for my man.

"Ooh, you look good," he smiled and pecked me.

"I do?" I frowned as I looked down at myself. I had on a big t-shirt, no pants, or makeup, and my hair was hanging loosely.

"Yeah, I love when you dress down," he replied and shut the front door.

"Thank you," I half smiled, as we walked and sat down on the couch simultaneously.

He reached over and grabbed the other half of my sandwich. He took a big ass bite before I could even protest.

"Deshawn! I wanted that part too!" I whined and slapped his arm.

"Baby, what's up with you? You've been eating like a damn cow," he chuckled.

"No I haven't!" I shouted.

"Whoa, you good?" he furrowed his brows.

"Yeah I'm fine, I just wanted both sandwiches." I smacked my lips and bit into the half that I still had.

"You never usually eat both babe. I'm sorry; I wouldn't have taken it if I knew. You want it back?" he asked.

"Yes!" I snatched it and bit into it. He stared at me with his eyes bucked. "What?" I spat. He burst into laughter, and I just stared at him confused. "Is something funny?" I asked with a mouthful of sandwich.

"You have mustard all over your face," he laughed.

"Oh," I responded as he wiped my face with the paper towel. He threw it into the wastebasket next to the couch, as I finished the last bite.

Once I was done, he placed his hand on my stomach and kissed me softly. "Why are you doing that?" I glared at him.

"Doing what Yuki?" he asked.

"Touching my stomach like that!" I turned my lip up.

"Like what? I'm just touching you. Kiyuki, what's wrong?" he quizzed as he searched my face for the answer.

"I'm late," I huffed.

"Late for what?" his dumb ass questioned.

"My period, Deshawn. It's late, a week late," I rolled my eyes.

"How late is it usually supposed to be?" he inquired.

"It's not supposed to be late at all fool!" I smacked the back of his head and shook mine.

Lord, if I'm pregnant, give the baby my brains, I said to myself.

"So you're having my baby," he grinned and touched my flat stomach.

"I'm not sure yet. It could still show up," I said smacking his hand off of me.

"Come on, let's go get a test." He hopped up off the couch.

"Right now? It's late," I looked up at him.

"Yes woman. Go get dressed," he ordered. I got up and pouted all the way to my room. I slipped on some tights, and then some slide-ins.

"Look at my pretty ass baby mama," Deshawn chuckled as I emerged from the back. I rolled my eyes, grabbed my jacket, and then we headed to the pharmacy.

We bought six different tests, just to make sure. "Why in the hell do them things cost so fucking much?" Deshawn frowned as I looked over the tests in the car.

"Babe, can you stop," I asked pointing to a McDonalds. He looked over at me, and then looked back to the road and laughed. "What's so funny?" I asked as he pulled into the drive thru.

"I'm not gone say shit, because you're already on edge," he said as he rolled the window down to order.

I got my meal, plus a sundae, and then we rushed home. I scarfed down my food, and then Deshawn damn near dragged me to the bathroom. My bladder seemed to be weak these days, and I'd just drank a load of pop so I had plenty of pee for the tests. I peed on three of them, and then he and I waited impatiently.

"I don't want to look," I said and got up to go into my bedroom.

"It's cool baby, I can read it." Deshawn replied as he studied the back of the box to make sure.

I sat down on my bed, and then decided to get on Instagram to pass the time, and to take my mind off it. I heard Deshawn coming down the hall, and I swallowed the lump in my throat. He walked slowly into my semi dark room, with a somber look on his face. I smiled inside because I knew what that meant - I wasn't pregnant. He neared me, and then stroked my hair.

"I can't wait to meet our baby." He bit his lip and then leaned down to kiss me passionately.

"Wait, what?" I pulled away and frowned. He took his right arm from behind his back, and showed me the three positive tests. "I'm pregnant?" I asked no one in particular.

"Yeah baby. Aren't you excited?" He kneeled down in front of me. *Hell no!* I thought.

"Yeah, yeah of course," I said instead. He raised my shirt and kissed my stomach gently.

"I love you Kiyuki Allen, and I'm gonna do everything I can to make sure you and my baby are always good," he said looking up into my eyes. That warmed my heart, and for a moment I smiled at the thought of being pregnant.

"I know," I whispered. He kissed me hard, and then we proceeded to make love to celebrate.

MAXIMILIAN

I found out Cobra's bitch ass was staying in some little secluded home in Ferndale. It was time I ended this nigga's life. Any muthafucka that will leave his mother and sister in the hands of his enemy, is not to be left living, regardless of anything else.

I didn't call Deshawn, because I didn't feel I needed help on this one. I wanted this killing all to myself, since I was mainly the one he fucked with. And to think this was all because of Cori's ass setting up all them damn robberies. I swear, as soon as I saw that bitch, she was getting a bullet to the dome.

I pulled up to the house, and I saw the TV light flickering in the living room. This nigga was living footloose and fancy free, while his family members were being held captive. I shook my head at my thoughts, as I exited the car. I walked around the side, and saw there was a big ass bay window in the back. I searched for a rock on the floor, and when I found one I busted the window open. I quickly climbed through, and hid in the closet when I heard footsteps enter the room.

"What the fuck?" I heard Cobra say as I watched him inspect the window through the closet shutters. "Fucking perras!" he said in a low tone as he exited the room.

I was about to step out of the closet, but I heard him return. He had some trash bags and duct tape with him, preparing to fix his window. He sat it down, and then rushed out as if he had forgotten something. I heard him searching the house, and then he finally came back. He sat his gun on the floor, and then pulled a long piece of duct tape from the roll. Just as he was taping the trash bag, I silenced my gun, slipped my arm out of the closet, and fired three shots into the back of his head. He fell forward, and slid onto the floor with his trash bag.

Since I had plastic on my shoes, a ski mask, and gloves, I walked out of the room and left out of the front door. I had already made sure no one was outside prior. I called my crew to come and clean the scene up for me, and then I drove to the warehouse.

After I arrived, I took a deep breath, and then walked inside. I went to the back room, and when I peeked in, his mother and sister, Esmeralda were asleep. I closed the door behind me, and both of their eyes popped open.

"I'm wondering if I should kill y'all or let you go," I said.

"Please let us go papi, we won't say a thing," Esmeralda replied.

I looked over at her fine ass, and then looked away to think some more. I hated killing people for no reason, but then I didn't need witnesses floating around.

"Yes, we will forget this all," her mother added after a couple seconds of silence. I sat down in the chair, and stared at them for a moment.

"Aight, look. I'm gone let y'all go, but I'm gone have somebody watching y'all from now until forever. If they even think that y'all are doing some shady shit, it's a wrap for y'all," I said.

I was gonna pay someone to simply follow them without them knowing who it was. That would be that person's only job. Both ladies nodded, so I stood up to untie them. The mother hugged me tightly, and then so did Esmeralda.

"Thanks papi," she said and kissed my cheek. The three of us walked out to the car, and I took them to their home.

"Won't you stay for some late breakfast?" his mother smiled when we pulled up to the house. I wanted to decline, but I did need them to stay on my side until their watchdog arrived. Plus, if she was willing to cook me a meal after being held hostage for days on end, how could I say no?

"Why not," I replied and shut my engine off.

Astrid, Cobra's mother, started the food, while Esmeralda went to clean herself up. I looked down at my phone, and nodded when I saw it was only 9:45pm.

As I waited for the food to cook, Esmeralda emerged from the bathroom in just a towel. She bit her full bottom lip, and then adjusted the towel giving me a quick view of her sexy ass body. I stared, and she smirked before walking off. My dick was hard as a rock in this moment. I rubbed my eyes to erase the memories of me fucking her in the past.

"I'm gonna take a quick shower while the quiche bakes," Astrid smiled and then walked off.

I looked around the living room taking in the atmosphere, and suddenly Esmeralda came out from the back wearing booty shorts and a crop top. Hips, ass, thighs, breasts, she had it all and a lot of it. *Lord give me strength,* I said to myself.

"Thank you for letting us go," she said as she sat next to me. Whatever soap she used smelled sweet and sexy.

"No problem," I nodded.

"I'm trying to think of a way to thank you," she whispered.

"You just did," I responded dryly.

"I don't think saying it is enough though," she said into my ear. Her minty breath made it tingle.

"Nah, you good," I replied.

"I wanna show you how much I appreciate you," she said as she planted a soft wet kiss on my neck.

"Chill out Esme." I moved away. "I'm married," I scoffed.

"You're only twenty-four, babe, why did you get married?" she frowned.

"Because I fell in love. Why else do people marry?" I shook my head.

"I understand. Well if she ever messes up, or if you want to lay up let me know," She said as she snatched my phone and typed her number in. "In case you lost it." She handed my phone back to me.

"How old are you again?" I asked. *Why are you asking Max? It doesn't matter*, I told myself.

"I'm twenty-four too remember?" she smiled. Lord she was beautiful.

"Oh, aight. Tell your mom I have to go, but thanks for the gesture," I said getting up.

I sped home, and talked my dick down. Once it was soft, I got out of the car and went inside to take a shower.

"You missed dinner," Namiko said when I walked into our dark bedroom.

"I know baby. I will be here for dinner tomorrow," I responded as I climbed into bed.

She was wearing panties and a bra. Her ass and titties had gotten plumper since the baby, and her hips spread some too. I loved that shit.

"Come here," I said as I climbed on top of her. I sucked her full lips, and released her plump round breasts. "These are beautiful babe," I whispered before hungrily sucking her nipples.

"Mmmm, Maxxxx," she purred.

Since I was already naked, I slipped her white lace panties down, and then flipped her over. I squeezed and bit her little fat ass, before slipping my fingers into her from behind. I plunged in and out of her, and licked her juices as they came rushing out.

"Uhhh, uhhh," she cried out. I latched onto her clit, and sucked it harder as I fingered her faster. "I'm cumming," she cooed as she creamed all over my fingers.

I slowly slipped them out of her, and sucked all her juices off. She turned over, and started sucking my dick like the little closet porn star that she was. I humped her face, as I massaged her scalp slowly.

"Fuck Namiko," I whispered as I bumped her tonsils.

She gagged a bit, and it turned me on even more. Her mouth was wet as hell, and saliva was dripping down her chin. *Got damn!*

"Swallow that shit." I bit my lip as I released down her throat. She swallowed it up, and then I pushed her back. I put her legs on my shoulders, and then slid into her warm, snug walls. "This my pussy," I said as I thrust into her hard and fast.

"Yes Max. It's your pussy," she whimpered while making the sexiest face.

I leaned down and bit her flat stomach, making sure not to break my stride. I slammed into her, and every time I pulled out, my dick was covered in her sweet cream.

"You always cum so hard for me," I grunted. "Cum for me again, just like that," I demanded as I leaned down and devoured her hard nipples.

"I'm cumming again, babe." She moaned loudly as I pinned her thighs back. I tugged on her lip with my teeth, as I plunged into her in a circular motion.

"This pussy is so good," I said in a low tone more so to myself, as I humped away.

"Uuhhhhh," we both yelled as we came again. I pinned her hands behind her head, and pecked her soft lips. I kissed from her neck to her stomach, and then laid on my back.

"Come sit on my face," I said.

"I'm tired," she pouted.

I tugged her over, and then positioned her pussy right into my mouth. I sucked, licked, and fingered her constantly until she came hard three times.

"Maaaxx, what are you doing to me?" she purred, as I positioned her above my dick.

"Ride it for daddy," I said as she began to rock her hips and bounce slowly.

"You gone start doing what I tell you?" I asked as I watched her titties bounce.

"Yes," she replied and stared me in the eyes with her pretty ass. I smirked and then flipped her on her back to beat that shit up again. This was gonna be a good long night.

NAMIKO

"Max, stop, I'm still sore from last night," I whispered as I felt his hands grab a handful of my ass.

His hands felt rougher than usual, and he didn't say anything, but kept groping me. He reached around and cupped my breasts, and when I looked down I didn't recognize the hands.

"What the fuck!" I jumped and turned over.

I saw Ms. Gwen's boyfriend Alfred smirking at me. I squirmed to the point where I fell off the edge of the bed.

"Relax baby girl," he smiled, flashing a couple of gold teeth.

"What are you doing in my bed?" I shouted.

"What do you think?" he chuckled and then got up.

His shirt was dingy as fuck, and his jeans were too. He stretched and scratched his big belly.

"You need to leave," I finally said standing up.

"Not until I get my money," he glared at me.

"Money? What money?" I frowned.

"Look, I know you know the combination to Max's safe. I just need to borrow a couple of dollars; actually a couple thousand," he said.

"I'm not giving you anything! How did you even get in my house?" I replied folding my arms.

"Got the key from Gwendolyn," he said as he dangled it in the air. I reached for it but he pulled away and cackled.

"Now you can give me the money, or give me some of you." He bit his crusty bottom lip, and ran his callous finger across my cheek. I slapped his hand down, and he immediately grabbed me by the shoulders. "I'm not fucking around with you little bitch! Either you can give me some pussy, or get me $10,000 from the safe in his office," he said through gritted teeth.

"Fine! I will get you the money." I turned my lip up at the smell of onions on his breath.

"Hurry up!" he hollered tossing me into the nightstand.

I pulled myself together, and then walked towards the bedroom door. I didn't even know the combination by heart; I'd always kept it in my phone. However, even if I did I wasn't giving him the money. He followed behind me as I walked slowly as hell down the staircase.

I paused for a second. "Let me go check on my baby really fast," I said attempting to stall so I could have time to think.

"Do it quick!" he spat, as he snatched me back up the stairs by my arm. I rubbed my sore bicep as I walked to baby Max's room. I peeked in and checked on him, and I guess I was taking too long because Alfred burst in.

"Let's go Natiko!" he shouted. This nigga knew how to pronounce my name.

"It's Namiko." I rolled my eyes and walked out the door past him. Once we neared the office, I thought of another stall tactic. "My key, I forgot my key to his office," I chuckled nervously.

"No, you're bullshitting me," he scowled and slammed me up against Max's wooden double doors. He ripped my gown open as I grabbed and pulled on his short hair. "Arrrhgghhhh!" he shouted and punched me in the stomach.

I kept my grip on his short hair, and pulled the hardest I could. Like a bitch, he reached up and pulled on my bun. I didn't even care that I was damn near naked. We spun around in constant circles as we pulled on each other's hair. His light skin tone started to turn bloodshot red, as I released one clump of hair to punch the side of his face.

"You little bitch!" he yelled, as I pulled on his hair with one hand, and punched his face repeatedly with the other.

I then kicked him in the nuts four times, causing him to release the grip he had on my bun and fall to the ground. I snatched a picture frame off the wall, and just as I was about to bust his ass over the head, I heard the front door slam.

"Namiko, what the fuck is going on?" Max frowned down at a groaning Alfred in confusion. He then looked at me and eyed my ripped open gown.

"I-he- he's crazy," was all I managed to get out.

Max walked closer to us, and towered over Alfred who was still sitting on the ground clutching his balls.

"Go change Nami," Max said without looking at me. I pieced my gown together like it was a robe, and then walked around the corner to eavesdrop.

"Fuck you doing in my crib nigga?" Max asked in a calm tone.

"I came to pick up some umm, sugar for Gwendolyn," he lied as he squinted up at Max. *Sugar? He couldn't do any better than that?* I rolled my eyes.

"Why are my wife's clothes ripped?" Max folded his arms. His dark caramel complexion reddened, indicating his anger.

"Hey, ain't my fault she tried to have a little something on the side," he joked.

"Namiko, come here," Max called out, obviously knowing I was near.

"Yes," I said.

"Did he try to fuck you?" he quizzed, as Alfred tried to stand to his feet.

"He groped me in our bed," I replied.

I wished I hadn't said that because Max immediately yelled for me to leave the hallway. I rushed away for real this time, and went to shower.

When I got out, I put on my lotion, brushed my teeth, and got dressed. I then did the same for my son. I fed baby Max, and as I started to prepare breakfast for Max and I, he walked into the kitchen.

"Where is Alfred?" I inquired.

"Gone," he chuckled.

"Gone home? Did you tell your mom?" I questioned.

"Nah, gone to his fucking maker," Max replied and left the kitchen.

I finished making breakfast, put MJ in his baby swing, and then called Max down to eat with me.

"You killed him?" I asked.

"Namiko, that's not something we should be talking about," he responded as he bit into his maple sausage.

"Where is the body?" I questioned.

"Namiko! I said we're not gonna discuss this! Eat your fucking food and think of a new topic!" Max shouted and banged on the table making me jump.

I picked my cup up, threw my juice in his face, and then stormed out of the dining room. I went into the den, and then cut on the TV while I looked over some flash cards for my political science test. Max came in right after, and he had juice dripping from his face. I bucked my eyes because he was panting angrily with his jaws clenched. He was so sexy, especially when he was all mad and shit. He walked over and leaned down close to my face before speaking.

"Namiko Davis, make that the last fucking time you disrespect me like that. I'm trying to protect you, and I can't do that when you try to know every damn thing I do. When I tell you a topic is not to be discussed, you need to respect me as your husband and do what the fuck I say. Now I could disrespect you like you did me, by fucking you up right now, but I love your bratty ass too much. So like I said, make that the first and last time you throw some shit in my face," he scowled, as juice dripped from his little chin hairs and onto my collarbone.

I nodded my head, and then kissed his full lips passionately. He reciprocated thank God, and fucked me roughly right there on the couch.

"You better start listening," he panted as he thrust into me hard and fast, while biting my shoulder.

"I will daddy," I whimpered, as he moved to devour my nipples hungrily. He sucked my lips gently, while going ham in between my hips, until we both climaxed.

ANIKU

For some reason, I kept thinking that Namiko would find out that I'd had sex with Konz. I told him to make sure he didn't say anything to his brother, because we all know married couples talk about everything. On the bright side, I loved being Konz's girl. He was so much fun, and everyday was like a new adventure it seemed.

"How was class?" Namiko asked as she prepared sandwiches for lunch.

"It was good, but I have to take my sandwich to go, Nami," I smiled.

"To go? I was hoping we could eat lunch together since you're always with Orianna," she pouted.

"I know, but umm, I have a project due and Orianna is on my team. We want to start right away," I lied and prayed she fell for it.

"Is this project involving Konz?" she asked as she laid the bacon in the skillet.

"No it doesn't. It's for umm, my drama class," I replied.

"Alright Aniku." She exhaled as she handed over my bacon, melted cheese, turkey, lettuce, and tomato sandwich. It was piping hot and I was ready to scarf this shit down.

"Thank you. Love you." I hopped up, kissed baby Max's cheek, and rushed out.

On the way to Konz's house, I ate my bomb ass sandwich, and then stopped at Starbucks for an iced tea. I parked my car in his little garage, and then banged on the door within it that led to the inside of the house.

"Damn babe," he chuckled as he pulled the door open.

"We need to get you a new car," he said as he eyed Namiko's old car that she'd given me. I ignored his statement, and kissed his lips while cupping his face. He picked me up, and then carried me to the bedroom.

"Konz, can we chill for a little bit first?" I frowned as he reached his hands under my dress.

"We can talk later; I want some pussy," he panted.

"Don't you think we have sex too much?" I quizzed.

"There is no such thing. And what did I tell you? I said as soon as you let me I was gonna be doing it to you all the time." He smiled as he pulled my dress over my head.

He flicked his tongue over my hard nipples, while playing with my clit. I spread my legs some more, and threw my head back.

"Ahhh, ahhh!" I cried out as he sped up his finger thrusts. "I'm about to cuumm," I whimpered as he sucked my nipple. "Uuhhhhhh!" I moaned as I came hard on his finger.

He pulled it out and sucked off my juices with his eyes closed. He stood up and undressed quickly. I admired his smooth brown skin, and his chiseled chest and abs. He dropped down, and began to suck my clit slowly. I ran my hands over his fresh fade, and cupped the back of his head as I ground my hips into his face.

"Shit, Konz," I purred. He stuck his tongue into my opening, and then collapsed his lips around my button. "Ugghhhhh," I grunted as I released. He pecked my lower lips, and then stood up.

His long thick dick stared me in the face, and I looked up at him. "I don't think I can do it well," I said.

"You'll learn," he replied, and poked at my lips with the tip. I opened my mouth, and he slowly started to hump my face. "Watch your teeth and don't swallow your spit," he panted. I did as he asked, and although my saliva was coming out in abundance, I didn't stop it. "Yes, Aniku. Just like- aww fuck," he whispered, as he pumped into my mouth in a circular motion. His encouraging words made me go harder and next thing I knew, a warm liquid was spilling into my mouth. "Take it down," he ordered and I swallowed it.

He turned me over, pushed my head down into the pillow, and made me toot my ass up. He spread my legs, and I listened to him open a condom. He started to slide into me, and I put my hand back to stop him.

"It hurts Konz," I whimpered. He slapped my hand out of the way, and plunged into me fully. He played with my clit, as he pounded into me roughly. "Uuhhhhh uhhhhh!" I screamed at the pain mixed with pleasure. He spanked my ass, and then reached under me to pinch my nipples while plowing into me. I quickly crawled away, making his dick slide out of me.

"The fuck is you doing?" he frowned down at me, with his big dick sticking straight out.

"I don't want to do it anymore," I replied as a tear slipped out of my eye. I wiped it almost as soon as it appeared.

"Why not?" he asked obviously upset.

"Because you're hurting me. You never make love to me," I started to cry.

He closed his eyes and exhaled heavily. He walked over to me on his knees, and then laid down between my legs. He cupped my face and kissed me nice and slow, while sucking my tongue and lips. He wiggled into me, and pumped me nice and slow. He reached on his nightstand, and cut the light off so that it was slightly dim in the room. He kissed on my lips, cheeks, neck, and collarbone while stroking me gently.

"This what you want?" he bit his lip as he stared down into my eyes. I nodded and he darted his tongue back into my mouth.

He bear hugged my body, sucked on my neck, and then pumped me in a circular motion, making me cum hard.

"Fuck. Shit," he huffed as he filled up the condom. He picked his head up, and kissed my lips gently. "I love you aight?" he smirked.

"I love you too," I giggled.

Afterwards, we took a shower together, and then picked out some movies to watch. We ordered pizza, and I let Namiko know I was staying with Orianna after letting Orianna know the deal.

"We don't have to make love all the time, just sometimes," I said.

"I know. I'm just not used to that shit, but I guess I have to get used to it, right?" he chuckled and I nodded.

Suddenly his phone rang, and I saw the name Jaleesa flash on it. He looked down and hit the red decline button on his iPhone.

"Who is she?" I asked.

"Nobody," he replied as he bit into the pizza slice.

"Why is she calling then?" I inquired.

"Cause I used to fuck her but I don't anymore," he responded dryly. "Look, quit tripping, I'm with you and nobody else," he added and pecked my lips.

"Okay," I sighed.

He powered his phone off, and then tossed it into the drawer. I kissed the corner of his mouth, and he smiled down at me. I prayed silently that I didn't make a mistake.

EVELYN TURNER

"Namiko, tell me what you know," I whined.

"All I know is that they're together, and from what Yuki tells me it's very serious. She's actually coming over tomorrow because she has news for Aniku and I," she replied.

"Oh my gosh." I slouched down on the couch and slapped my hand onto my forehead. "Has Max told you anything?" I asked.

"No, nothing," she shrugged.

"She doesn't even want him Namiko. You know she's just dating him to get back at me!" I yelled.

"Maybe Ev, but it doesn't seem that way," she frowned.

"I have to go," I said standing up.

"Where are you going? I thought we were gonna study for the political science test," she frowned in confusion.

"Tomorrow, I promise. I have something to do," I replied and rushed out of the den.

I sped home, and rushed inside to call Deshawn. I needed to get him over here so I could talk to him. We never really discussed how he and Kiyuki became this item, and I needed answers.

"Hey," he answered and a smile crept across my face.

"Hey, I was wondering if you could come over to talk," I said and stared at the ceiling awaiting his response.

"For what Ev?" he asked.

"I just need some closure Deshawn. We broke up so abruptly and I just need to close our chapter," I responded and hoped that was a good enough explanation.

"Aight, I'll stop by there around seven," he sighed.

"Okay, see you soon," I smiled and disconnected the call.

I wasn't really sure what happened between us. We were good, and then all of a sudden, this home wrecking hoe just up and steals him. I don't even know how she was able to do it, but hoes stay winning I see. What the fuck did she have that I didn't? Whatever.

I climbed out of bed, and pulled some pork chops down from the freezer to thaw out. While that took place, I went and ran me a bubble bath using my Bath and Body Works bubbles. The clock read 5pm on the dot, so I knew I needed to hurry up and have everything set to get my man back. I wanted to show him how good it was to be with me.

After my bath, I fried up the pork chops, made some yams, and then some rice as well. I made a chocolate cake too, and by the time I was done it was 6:50pm.

"Shit," I said as I rushed to the back room.

I sprayed on my perfume, slipped into some lingerie, and then perfected my short curly bob. I prepared our plates, and then waited for my love to get here.

DING!

DONG!

I jumped at the sound of the bell, and then hopped up to answer the door. I closed my silk robe, because I wanted my attire to be a surprise.

"Hey what's up?" Deshawn smiled and hugged me.

"What's all this?" he chuckled as he looked around the living room. I had candles lit, and Monica playing low on the speakers.

"You hungry?" I cheesed.

"Umm, I could eat," he replied after looking at his watch. I grabbed his big hand, and led him to the kitchen. "Damn, it smells good in here Ev," he said as he put his nose up to sniff. The yams smelled sweet, just the way he liked them. "Pork chops, and you fried them too," he nodded and smiled, as I set the plate in front of him. I sat across from him, and we said grace before digging in.

"I bet you haven't had this meal in a while," I smirked.

"Nope, I've been working." He shook his head as he scooped some rice into his mouth.

"I used to cook for you every night," I said as I sipped my glass of wine.

"Yeah, you did," he replied scarfing down his food.

"You miss my food?" I asked.

"Sometimes," he responded.

"It could be like this again ya know." I bit my lip as he looked at me.

"How so?" he raised a brow.

"If you come back home," I smiled and rubbed his hand.

"Ev, come on now," he sighed.

"What? I miss you baby," I whined. He dropped his fork and finished chewing his food, before sipping his pop. "You don't ever miss me?" I cocked my head.

"I mean, I was with you for a while so yeah, sometimes I find myself missing little things about you, but I'm in love with someone else," he said.

"In love? You haven't even been with her a year. How are you in love already?" I frowned.

"I just am. Time has nothing to do with it. I know people who got married after knowing each other only two weeks, and it lasted forever," he shrugged.

"Deshawn, what about me? You're just gonna leave me and that's it?" I started to cry.

"Ev, please don't cry babe." He exhaled and walked over to me. "In a perfect world I would have the both of you, but I can't. I had to choose, and-"

"You chose her? Are you crazy? She's a fucking hoe! A low down dirty ass hood rat! There are so many hustlers that have fucked her it's ridiculous!" I shouted. "Does she even have walls?" I laughed wryly.

"I don't care about none of that. All I care about is how she is now and in this moment." He folded his arms.

"What type of nigga wants a hoe for a girlfriend?" I scoffed.

"Me! I do! I love her ass too! And I don't want you!" he pointed in my face.

"Oh, now you don't want me? You're not a real man, Deshawn. If she was able to just come and steal you from your happy home, you're weak as hell!" I yelled.

"Happy home? How in the fuck can you call this a happy home, Evelyn? Was it when you were jumping down my throat for me texting my own damn cousin? Or was it when the nurse had to stop you from putting your hands on me, while I was laid up in the hospital fresh from a coma? Which one, because none of this has been a happy home lately!" he hollered.

"Deshawn, don't do this," I sniffled.

"I didn't want to hurt you but I had to choose," he said in a low tone.

"Maybe you don't," I replied and even surprised myself. But maybe if he dated us both, I could eventually get him away from Kiyuki.

"Ev, what kind of shit is that? Have some respect for yourself baby girl. You're a good woman; don't stoop to the side chick level. Not for me or any other nigga," he replied squinting his sexy eyes.

I ignored his reply, and opened my robe. I dropped it to the floor, and cheesed as he took in my thick ass body. He leaned down and picked my robe up. He draped it over my body, and held it closed. I was so fucking embarrassed. No nigga had ever turned down pussy from me.

"I'm gonna pretend this never happened for your sake." He shook his head as I stared up at him.

"So we're done? It's over?" I sobbed.

"Yeah," he replied and turned to leave.

"Just give me a chance to show you that I've changed!" I called after him.

"She's having my baby Evelyn, it's over," he responded in a concerned tone, as if he was pleading for me to stop my antics.

I couldn't even say anything, because what he'd just said felt like someone had stuck a dagger into my chest.

"Thanks for the food, and have a goodnight," he added and left. I dropped onto the floor, and cried my eyes out.

KIYUKI

Tonight, Deshawn and I were going to a birthday party for a friend of his and Max's. I wasn't really in the mood to go, because I'd been sick as hell these past few weeks, but I decided to put on my big girl panties and attend anyway. Plus, I knew everybody who was anybody was gonna be there, and I wanted all these bitches to know that Deshawn was mine.

I wore a simple red dress, with matching red pumps. I put my long hair into a side braid, and then put on my gold hoops.

"You look sexy, babe." Deshawn peeked his head into the room.

"Thank you," I smiled, and pecked him lightly so that my lipstick wouldn't rub off on him.

He wore a black button up, with black slacks and shoes to match. He smelled good as hell as usual, and I couldn't wait to walk into the party on his arm. He leaned down and kissed my flat stomach, then we headed out.

We pulled up to a venue located on Monroe Street, and there were so many people hanging around outside. Some people were dressed to impress and some were looking a fucking mess. After parking the car, my baby came around and opened the door for me, before helping me out. I loved that he always did that.

We walked up to the front, and Deshawn gave the bouncer his name. You could hear "Shaka Zulu" by Tyga blasting from outside. We walked in and it was packed wall to wall with people shaking their asses.

"It's so loud," I whispered into Deshawn's ear and he laughed. Once we spotted the VIP section that Namiko and Max were in, we headed up there.

"What's up man?" Max dapped Deshawn up.

"Kiyuki," he said and hugged me. Max was dressed in all black like Deshawn, except he wore a black bowtie as well.

"Hey," I smiled and looked around the section before hugging my little sister.

After dancing to a couple songs, I decided I would go and sit down. I felt tired as hell, and I was starving too. As I bobbed my head to the music, I saw Evelyn walk into the VIP area. She approached Namiko, Max, and Deshawn giving them all hugs. I kept my eye on her because I was sure that she wasn't over Deshawn yet. Shit, if he dicked her down the way he did me I knew she wasn't willing to let that go.

"Jersey" by Drake and Future came on and when Namiko started to dance on Max, Evelyn started to grind her ass on my nigga. I hopped up off the little couch, and stormed over to them. I snatched Deshawn's arm and glared up at his stupid ass.

"Is there a problem?" Evelyn frowned and folded her arms across her big breasts.

"Yeah, I don't want you dancing on my man," I replied.

"Your man? Bitch please, last time I checked he was mine and you stole him!" she shouted over the music.

"Doesn't matter how I got him, but in this moment in time he's mine," I raised a brow.

"Tell her!" I shouted to Deshawn.

"Kiyuki, you already-"

"You know what, fuck you. She can have you." I shook my head and walked down the stairs of VIP.

"Kiyuki! Kiyuki!" I heard him shouting after me.

"Deshawn! Deshawn, come back here!" Evelyn called after him.

The three of us walked out and ended up in the parking lot. I walked to the passenger side of Deshawn's car when I remembered he drove us.

"Yo, what's wrong with you? Come back inside," he frowned.

"No, I'm hungry, I'm tired, and I'm done with you. Just take me home," I spat.

"You ain't done with nobody girl," he said pulling me close.

"Deshawn! Really?" Evelyn yelled, as she got closer to us. I wanted to fuck her up again, but my baby's life was more important than her and Deshawn.

"Evelyn, take yo' ass on somewhere!" Deshawn hollered.

By now, the people waiting to get into the venue were staring hard and gathering around.

"Oh, so she's more important than me now?" Evelyn quizzed.

"Yes Ev! I love her and she's having my baby! Take yo' ass back inside or something!" he shouted across the parking lot as the bystanders made comments. Evelyn shook her head at him as tears rolled down her cheeks.

"You said I could be on the side," she sobbed looking pathetic as fuck.

"On the side?" someone yelled and smacked their lips.

"Evelyn, you tripping right now," Deshawn scoffed and hit his alarm to unlock the car doors.

"No nigga *you* tripping! This ain't over!" she yelled and ran back through the crowd of people.

On the way home I didn't say a word, until I realized we weren't going to my house. "Take me home Deshawn," I said as we pulled into the driveway of that new house he bought.

"Shut up and get out," he laughed. I didn't budge, so he came around, opened the door, and then lifted me out bridal style.

"Put me down!" I whined as he carried me to the front door. He put me on my feet while he unlocked the door, then scooped me right back up as we went inside. The place was now fully furnished and was gorgeous.

"Deshawn, this is beautiful," I whispered as I took it all in.

"I know, and this is our home babe," he said as he put me down and hugged me from behind.

"I can't leave my parents' house. It has sentimental value," I replied.

"Well, I will pay the mortgage on it to keep it, but you can live here with me." He kissed my neck and I smiled.

"I can't wait to spend Thanksgiving and Christmas here," I said in a low tone. It was the middle of October so the holidays were close.

"Yeah, all we need are some cheesy Christmas pictures to hang on the walls," he joked, and we laughed. "I'm sorry I didn't immediately check Evelyn back at the club," he said, turning me to face him.

"Yeah, you better not do that again," I glared at him playfully.

"I won't. And you better not try to leave me or even say that you will. Especially not with my baby in your stomach," he said.

"Well if you keep up all this good stuff, we will be good," I smiled. I cupped his face and we indulged in a passionate kiss. "I love you," I whispered.

"I love you too baby," he bit his sexy lip.

MAXIMILIAN

"Mr. Davis, your mother is here," our new nanny and maid, Dorothea, peeked her head into my office.

"Thanks," I sighed.

I'd been avoiding my mom ever since I had to body her boyfriend. I knew that she knew something was up, and that's why she was blowing up my phone. I wasn't in the mood to discuss him, and frankly I didn't care about his ass either. He deserved what happened to him for disrespecting my mother all these years and then putting his hands on my wife.

"Maximilian, where is Alfred?" she asked with tears sitting in her eyes.

"That's *your* boyfriend, shouldn't you know?" I raised a brow.

"Don't play stupid! I know you did something to him!" she shouted.

"You don't know anything, Ma. What would make you think I made him disappear? I've never made him disappear before," I squinted my eyes.

"Because, I gave him the key to come over here," she had to admit. "And he never came home," she added.

"Why would you give him a key to my crib?" I quizzed. I knew after Namiko changed the locks, I shouldn't have given her shit.

"He needed money and you were too selfish to just give it to him!" she yelled.

"Do you hear yourself? He was no good for you," I said standing up.

"You don't dictate who is good for me Maximilian Davis!" she hollered and pushed me with all her might.

"Are you hungry? Namiko is making lunch," I smiled. She scowled up at me and shook her head.

"Since you think you can dictate who I deal with, I can do the same," she smirked and turned on her heels.

Just as she was about to open my office door and walk out, Namiko came walking in with a tray of food for me.

"Oh, excuse me. Hello Ms. Gwen," she beamed looking beautiful as ever. She wore a simple blue dress, showing her small but sexy figure. Her beautiful dark caramel complexion glowed, and her slanted honey eyes were bright as the sun.

"Mhm, whatever," my mother waved her off and shoulder bumped her. Namiko slightly lost her balance when she was bumped, but tightened her grip on my tray of food.

"Here you go honey," she forced a smile as my mom left.

"Sorry about that beautiful," I said as I sat down in front of my food.

"Is she mad- I-I made dessert," she replied.

"What were you gonna ask?" I inquired.

"I'm staying out of it," she nodded. "Like we talked about," she smiled.

"Just ask me baby," I chuckled. "Is she mad about Alfred?" she bucked her eyes.

"Yeah, but she doesn't know anything. She's just guessing so keep your pretty mouth shut," I said.

"Of course daddy," she smiled, and pecked me with her full pouty lips.

"I'll bring you dessert once I feed and bathe MJ," she said as she switched off.

I shook my head because having a baby had definitely given her some sexy ass curves and a plumper ass.

"Damn," I said to myself as she left out.

Two Weeks Later...

Today, Namiko, Dorothea and I were flying to Jamaica to relax. Dorothea was lucky because she was getting a free trip all because of MJ. We only needed her to watch him at certain times so that she would be able to enjoy herself too. We were staying at Secrets Wild Orchid in Montego Bay, Jamaica, and the hotel was big as fuck.

"This is gorgeous Mr. Davis," Dorothea smiled as she climbed out of the van that drove us here.

"Yeah babe," Namiko whispered as she adjusted MJ on her hip.

As soon as we walked in, we were greeted with a towel and mimosas, which Namiko and Dorothea gladly took. Mimosas weren't for niggas like myself, so I declined. We checked into our rooms, and by that time MJ was knocked out.

KNOCK!

KNOCK!

I walked to the hotel door and looked through the peephole to see Dorothea. "I can hang here with baby Max if you guys want to go out." She smiled as I let her in.

"Yeah, we were gonna go chill on the beach," Namiko grinned. I love seeing my baby happy.

"Great, I have a book I will read until he wakes up," Dorothea replied as she sat down.

Namiko went to change into a very revealing two-piece bathing suit that I didn't even know she had. She looked good as hell, and I was thanking God that she was all mine. She pulled her hair up into a bun, and then reached for my hand.

"Let's go," she said. I looked downward as she pulled me, to watch her little round ass jiggle slightly. "Ow!" she whined, when I smacked and grabbed a handful of it as we walked down the hall.

"The stuff I'm gonna do to that tonight." I shook my head at my nasty thoughts.

It appeared to be a slow time of the year for the resort, so there were plenty of places for us to sit. We sat down on two of the comfy lounge chairs, and watched the pretty water wash up onto the shore.

"Thank you for this, babe," Namiko said and climbed into the chair with me.

"What you doing all in my space?" I smiled and welcomed her into my lap.

"Cause I like being as close as I can to you," she smirked.

"You look sexy as fuck in this little shoe string you got on," I joked.

"Thank you. I wanted to show people that you can look good after having a baby," she chuckled.

"Well you're showing 'em baby girl," I raised both brows.

After relaxing on the beach for a bit, we came back to the room to relax with MJ, while Dorothea explored Jamaica a bit. Once she returned, Namiko and I got dressed to go have dinner. Namiko wore a white dress that was long in the back and short in the front, complemented with gold accessories. I wore all black, which was my favorite color if you can call it that, and my Cartier watch and bracelet.

"You're so sexy husband." Namiko kissed my lips and made sure her lipstick wasn't on my lips.

"I know," I smirked and she hit me on the arm playfully.

We went to the restaurant, which was like in the middle of the water. It was really romantic but it was kind of scary because we all know black people and water don't mix.

"So, how is school going?" I asked as we sipped our drinks.

"It's going pretty good. I did better on my political science test than I expected," she replied.

"That's good baby, you only have a year and a half before you graduate," I smiled.

"Yeah, and I can't wait. But then I still have to continue so I can get the job I want," she sighed.

"I know it's a lot of work but that check will be worth it, babe." I kissed the back of her hand.

"I know. I know. So when you first saw me what did you think?" she cheesed.

"Where did this come from?" I chuckled as the waitress set down our plates.

"I just want to know," she grinned.

"Well, obviously I thought you were beautiful but also a little awkward," I laughed.

"Awkward?" she squealed.

"Yeah, you were kind of weird, but it was in a cute way. Then I got to know you and realized that you weren't weird at all. Daddy just made you nervous," I winked.

"Oh please!" she waved me off as she put a piece of jerk chicken into her mouth. "I was only awkward because of the job I was doing," she added.

"Woman, you were stuttering over your words when I first spoke to you," I chuckled.

"Fine, I'm busted. But so what, I was intrigued and had never been in the presence of someone so fine and with such a commanding demeanor," she responded.

"Well, I had never been in the presence of someone so beautiful and smart that wasn't just trying to come up off of a rich nigga," I said honestly. "I want you to know that I love you and MJ so much, and more than anything in this world. You two are the most important people in my life," I nodded.

"More important than work?" she asked.

"More important than any and everything," I reiterated and she smiled.

As soon as we got to the room, I couldn't keep my hands off of her. I'd text Dorothea earlier and told her to take MJ to her room for the night. Namiko and I kissed hungrily as we undressed down to nothing. I laid her sexy body down, and just took my time to admire her nakedness like always. I grabbed her small, but firm, round titties, and flicked my tongue over her hard nipples.

"Mmmm," she moaned as she arched her back.

I sucked harder, and then rubbed between her legs to see how ready she was. Once she was sopping wet, I dipped down between her legs and licked up her sweet juices.

"You taste so good Nami," I whispered in between licking and sucking on her clit.

"Ohhhh Max, babe," she purred and caressed my head. "Ooohhh," she grunted softly as she released into my mouth.

I licked her clean, and then went right back to sucking while thrusting my finger into her. Her pussy was so pretty, and my dick got harder and harder as I watched my fingers go in and out of her opening.

"Uhh, uhhh!" she cried out and came on my fingers.

I licked between her slit, and then slowly took my fingers out to lick them as well. I stood up, and Namiko immediately took my rod into her warm mouth. She massaged my balls, and sloppily sucked me up just the way I liked it.

"Damn Nami," I said in a low tone as I looked down at her. She worked her jaws up and down my shaft, letting her saliva coat it completely.

"Cum in my mouth daddy," she said in the freakiest little voice, making my balls tighten. Soon after, I exploded down her throat. "Mmmm." She licked her full lips after she swallowed.

"Turn your freaky ass around." I smiled and spanked her ass as she got on all fours.

She laid her head on the pillow, and stuck her plump derriere in the air. I kissed her pussy from the back, and then forced my way into her tight ass walls.

"Uhhhhhh, Maxx," she whimpered as I slowly pumped her in a circular motion.

I watched her ass jiggle every time I pumped, and I knew I'd be cumming soon. I reached my hand under and played with her clit as I started to beat it up.

"Oooh, ooohhh, oooohh," she screamed as she bit the pillow with her perfect set of teeth.

"Cum on your dick Nami," I whispered, just as she creamed on my dick.

I continued playing with her button while stroking her walls, and she came two more times back to back. I laid down, and she mounted me to ride. She wound her hips and bounced on my rod at a medium pace, giving me full view of her sexy body. I watched her toned stomach muscles contract, as sweat ran down between her perfect, perky breasts. We grabbed each other's hands and intertwined our fingers as she bounced a little faster.

"Fuck, ahh!" I called out as I felt my nut rising. "Work that shit Namiko," I grunted. It was feeling way too good.

"I'm cumming Max," she cooed as she rained down on me.

"Mmmm," I moaned as I shot my seeds up inside her.

She panted a little before collapsing onto me, and crushing her lips against mine. I sucked her lips and let our tongues dance for a couple minutes before we started round two.

NAMIKO

TWO WEEKS LATER

Regardless of how crazy Gwendolyn was, I wanted to make sure she was okay. I didn't want to have beef with my mother-in-law. Although Alfred was a piece of shit ass nigga, I knew she loved him and was probably miserable.

Against my better judgment, I decided to drop by her home and check on her. As I strutted up her walkway, I saw Deshawn's little brother, Robbie coming out of her home.

"How you doing Nami?" he licked his lips and folded his arms. I swear he looked just like Al B Sure's son; he and Deshawn.

"I'm doing okay. How are you?" I asked still confused as to why he was over Gwendolyn's house.

"I'm great, you're looking good this afternoon," he said as he neared me. I backed up once he got too close.

"Robbie, what are you doing here at Gwendolyn's?" I inquired.

"Just checking on her, you know she's like a second mother to Deshawn and I. Our mom is down in Alabama, ya know," he nodded.

"Oh, well nice seeing you," I said and started to walk past him.

"Come through the hood to see me some time," he smiled and grabbed my arm.

I snatched my arm from him and walked up to the door. I heard him chuckle then get into his car.

"Who is it?" Gwendolyn spat after I knocked on her door. *Fuck, she's in a shitty mood*, I thought.

I was about to turn and walk away, but the door flung open. "Oh, it's you," she smacked her lips and sauntered back into the house.

"Yeah, how are you?" I asked as I walked in behind her and closed the door.

"How do you think I am? That husband of yours killed the love of my life!" she shouted.

"We don't know that Ms. Gwen. Maximilian doesn't care enough about Alfred to do something like that," I said as I sat down next to her. I tried to rub her back, but she shot up off the couch and sat on the love seat.

"Don't touch me. I'm sure it was your fault. You've always had a thing for Alfred," she scowled.

"Are you kidding me? Come on now, I don't even see why *you* like Alfred," I laughed as she glared at me.

"You may be fooling Maximilian, Ms. Namiko, but you're not fooling me. I know you're nothing but a gold digging whore, trying to bleed my baby dry. Brainwashing him to believe all these bad things about me, while you blow his money on shopping trips and vacations to Jamaica!" she spat as she lit a cigarette. I'd never seen her smoke before, and didn't know she partook in it.

"Ms. Gwen, I love your son very much and I want to love you too. Why can't you understand that? I have no malicious intentions," I pleaded.

"No need to kiss my ass. You've had a baby so you're set for life. We may need to have a DNA test ran on that little fucker though," she chuckled, and flicked some cigarette ashes into the ashtray.

"Don't call my son names, Ms. Gwen. You can say whatever you want about me, but don't bring baby Max into this," I frowned. She was pissing me off.

"Or what? Huh? What the fuck are you gonna do if I talk about your precious little meal ticket?" she smiled.

"I don't want to but I will fuck you up," I stated calmly. She burst into laughter but I didn't budge.

"Watch your fucking mouth!" she yelled and stood up. *Here we go again*, I thought and stood up as well.

She went to the kitchen and came back with something to drink. I sat down once I realized she wasn't about to get rowdy with me. She sipped her drink and stared me down. I stared back because there was nothing else to look at honestly.

"Excuse me," I said as I got up and went to the bathroom. I went and used the restroom and then washed my hands. Once I was done, I stared at myself in the medicine cabinet mirror. "Be calm Namiko," I told myself. I took a deep breath and turned to leave the bathroom.

"Ahhhhhhhhhhh!" Gwendolyn burst into the bathroom screaming with a big ass knife in the air.

"Ms. Gwen what are you doing?" I hollered as she swung the knife at me.

"My son took Alfred away and now I'm gonna take you away!" she grunted and stabbed the wall, barely missing me.

I grabbed her wrists, and we tussled for a bit before falling into the tub and bringing down the shower curtain and rod. I grabbed the hand holding the knife, and banged it hard up against the shower wall repeatedly until the knife dropped. I quickly grabbed it and climbed out of the tub.

"You're fucking nuts!" I panted holding the knife in my hand.

She glared up at me while groaning because of her sore wrist. I was so tired of fighting Maximilian's family members. What the fuck! I walked out and took the knife into the kitchen.

"Uh!" I felt Gwendolyn wrap her arm around my throat trying to choke me.

We danced around the kitchen as I clawed at her forearm. I was starting to feel light headed from her cutting off my oxygen.

"Max is too good for you. Life was better before you came," she sobbed into my ear as my head throbbed.

I spotted a glass of orange juice on the table, and quickly grabbed it. I was getting weaker and weaker, and struggling to breathe.

"Arrgghhhhh!" she screamed as I bashed the glass against her cheek.

She immediately let me go, and grabbed her bloody face. I ran past her, out the house, and hopped in my car to go home. This was the last straw. I hated to do it, but unless that bitch got some professional help, Max needed to choose.

I knew he was at Red Sugar around this time, so I drove straight there. I rushed inside and straight up to his office. When I burst in, I saw the chick Claudia from school and some other girl sitting on his couch.

"Hey babe, these are the girls that replaced you and Kiyuki, Claudia and Aubrey," Max said.

"Don't I know you?" Claudia cocked her head to the side.

"I think from Wayne State," I panted.

"Right! The whole coffee grounds thing," she chuckled lightly.

"Ladies, can I talk to my husband please," I fake smiled.

"Oh, so you're Max's wife? I was wondering who she was," Claudia grinned and stood up.

"Yes, I am," I replied growing irritated.

She and the other chick walked out, and I closed the door quickly almost clipping Claudia's heel.

"What's up beautiful?" Max smiled and licked his full caramel lips.

"Your mother just tried to kill me! Again!" I cried.

"What? How? When?" he frowned.

"Like twenty minutes ago Max! She pulled a knife on me and then almost choked me out! I had to bust her ass over the head with a glass!" I yelled.

"Okay, calm down baby," he said as he hugged my body tightly. My small body melted into his strong embrace.

"I can't do this anymore Max. I'm tired of fighting her. She needs to get help or she can't come around me and the baby," I sniffled looking up at him.

"I know. I got you," he said looking at my bruised neck. He kissed my neck, and squeezed my butt roughly. He reached between my legs from the back, and rubbed my pussy through my panties.

"No. Take care of your mother," I spat and pushed him off.

"I will, right after I get some pussy," he said and lightly pushed me onto the couch.

EVELYN

I sat outside Deshawn's new home, drinking Jameson whiskey straight from the bottle. This shit was nasty as hell, but it was the only liquor strong enough to numb my fucking pain.

How could he do this to me? I did nothing wrong! I may have been a little insecure at times, but so what! He knew all my exes had cheated on me, and that it was gonna take some getting used to for me to trust him. He had no problem with that when we got to know each other on that Vegas trip.

I couldn't help but feel like he used me. This is exactly why I didn't like them light-skinned niggas! They always did bitches dirty because they thought they could, but not me.

"Ughck!" I shouted as I took another swig of the Jameson. It burned as it went down, and I was sure I had hair on my chest by now.

I didn't even know what I was doing out here. This was the fourth day in a row that I had sat outside his home until around 9am. After that, I would go to class, maybe study with Namiko, then come back here and sit outside. I watched as he and Kiyuki shopped for baby things, and even saw them kissing in the kitchen as she fried pork chops like I used to do for him. I also watched them fuck on top of the dryer in their little laundry room two days ago, and it made me sick.

I put the bottle of whiskey to my lips, but stopped when I saw Deshawn come out of the house with a bag of trash. He had on sweatpants and no shirt, looking sexy as hell. I climbed out of the car, and almost fell. I jogged over to him as fast as I could, calling his name.

"Evelyn? What the hell are you doing over here?" he frowned as he stopped me from falling.

"Deshawn, I love you," I slurred as tears ran down my cheeks.

"Evelyn, are you drunk? Please tell me you didn't drive over here like this." He shook his head in disappointment.

"Shut up! You're worried about the wrong thing!" I shouted.

"Evelyn, be quiet, it's late as hell," he whispered angrily.

"I don't give a fuck! I only care about you! Can't you see! I need you back or I'm gonna kill myself!" I screamed with my head back. I was so dramatic.

I heard his front door open, and there stood Kiyuki. The small bulge in her stomach only infuriated me further.

"Baby, go back inside, it's cold," Deshawn ordered.

"Are you okay?" Kiyuki asked.

"Just go inside Yuki!" he yelled. She paused and then did as she was told.

"Lap dog," I scoffed and took a swig of my drink.

"That's your fucking problem Ev. You're so busy making sure that no one tells you what to do, that you don't know how to let a man be a fucking man!" he said.

"I'm not gonna let a man boss me around!" I slurred and took another sip from the bottle.

"It's not about bossing you around. I didn't want to boss you around; I wanted you to respect the decisions I made when I felt it was what was best for us. I didn't mind you speaking your mind, but arguing with me and disrespecting me to get your point across was your problem. I want to be with a woman, not another nigga," he replied snatching the bottle from me, as I was about to sip from it.

"Okay, I get it now," I half smiled and moved closer to him.

"Yeah, but it's too late. I'm in love with someone else," he shrugged. "Now come on, I'm gonna drive you home," he said turning around.

"No, fuck that," I spat and headed towards my car.

He grabbed my arm but didn't tighten his grip in time, so I slipped away. Tears cascaded down my face as I rushed and got into my car.

"Evelyn! Open this fucking door! You're too fucking twisted to drive!" he shouted and banged on my window.

"Fuck you! You don't care about me!" I sobbed.

"Evelyn, I love you. Just because I'm not in love doesn't mean I don't care! Please open the door." He tugged on the door handle but it was locked.

"I need you to be *in* love with me," I cried hysterically and cranked up the car. He ran in front of it and put his hands on the hood.

"Stop Evelyn!" he yelled.

"I need you to love me!" I hollered at the top of my lungs.

"I'm in love with you baby," he said flashing his perfect white teeth. "Just please get out the car."

I smiled for a second until I realized he was playing me. "You lie!" I screamed and pressed my foot on the gas to scare him.

I thought it was still in park but it was in drive. Deshawn flew onto my hood and rolled onto the ground. *Oh fuck!* I thought as I looked at him laying in the middle of the street through my side mirror. His neighbor's porch lights started to come on, so I sped out of there. I drove straight to Namiko's, because she was the only person I could talk to.

"Hello?" she answered her phone.

"Come outside," I cried.

"What?"

"Just come outside!" I shouted.

"Okay, okay," she whispered and disconnected.

"What's going on Ev?" she asked as she slid into my car.

"I think I killed Deshawn," I said in a low tone.

MAXIMILIAN

We'd made a lot of money tonight at Red Sugar, and it was starting to become a pattern. Every night we seemed to make more money than the previous.

I shut down my computer, and then locked all my drawers. It was midnight and the club was still jumping, so I knew extra money would be coming in, on top of where we were at right now. A smile crept across my face at the thought.

My phone started to ring and I saw Namiko's name flash across. "Hey pretty," I sang into the phone.

"Max, something bad happened to Deshawn. Get home now!" she cried and told Evelyn to calm down.

"Something bad like what?" I frowned and grabbed my jacket.

"I don't know. I've been calling Kiyuki but she's not answering," she replied.

"Aight, I'm on my way," I said and hung up.

I turned my office light off, and then rushed outside to the back employee parking lot.

POW!

A gunshot rang out as I pushed the unlock button on my car remote. A sharp pain shot through my shoulder blade and I realized I was bleeding. I looked up from my wound, and couldn't believe my eyes.

POW!

Another shot pierced through my other shoulder.

POW!

A third one pierced my rib cage. My shirt was soaked in blood and my legs collapsed under me.

"Ma! Ma! Stop!" I shouted to my mother as she stood over me with the gun pointed in my face.

"Why did you take him, Max?" she sobbed as snot ran from her nose. I couldn't believe this shit; my own mother.

"Ma, don't do this. I'm your son. I'm more important than him," I pleaded with her.

"No, not anymore. All you care about is Namiko, so no you're not more important to me anymore," she smirked and pulled the trigger once more.

CORI SINEAD

I was at the airport getting ready to fly back to Michigan. I needed to get out of there for a while because that bitch Kiyuki caused me to lose my sanity damn near. After shooting at her, I knew the last little bit of marbles I had were gone. That's when I decided to go home to Alabama.

I made my mother promise not to tell Deshawn or Robbie where I was, because I knew they'd tell Max. At first she protested, but when I said they might take my life, she quickly changed her mind. Now that I was feeling better mentally, it was time to take Kiyuki down.

Deshawn told my mother that he'd met someone and was in love. When my mom told me it was Kiyuki, I became furious. How dare she try and sabotage my life, then try to run off into the sunset with my brother. I didn't care if she was pregnant; she was going the fuck down. Not only was she gonna lose Deshawn, but she was gonna lose her sister, too, once she found out that Kiyuki was behind all that bullshit. I was gonna have a harder time convincing Namiko, but I would make sure I had stone cold proof beforehand. Deshawn was my brother so proving to him that Kiyuki put a hit out on him and Max would be a piece of cake. Kiyuki Allen would regret the day that she ever fucked with me.

"Boarding first class!" the flight attendant called out over the airport. I got up and rushed over to have my ticket scanned. Shit was about to get way too real.

Become a VIP Reader!

*To join my mailing list text **SHVONNE** to **66866** and stay up to date! Also, join **Shvonne Latrice Reading Group** on Facebook!*

www.ingramcontent.com/pod-product-compliance
Lightning Source LLC
Chambersburg PA
CBHW061351310726
48974CB00001B/293